Mother Goose

The Carnival of Tales

a novella
by
John Passfield

Rock's Mills Press
Rock's Mills, Ontario • Oakville, Ontario
2023

Cover image: John Passfield
Cover design: Craig Passfield

Author's Website: www.johnpassfield.ca

For information, including permissions and bulk/retail purchases, please contact the publisher at customer.service@rocksmillspress.com.

Chapter 1

The nearby town of Binbrook. Pulling into the day-care driveway. Thanking the lady – Tammie – and buckling my granddaughter into the baby-seat in the car.

Ba Ba Black sheep have you any wool?

It gives me a break from all that writing. Something to get me out of the house. I plunge back into the stream and make my way.

There were two celestial children

A man driving a car.
A child singing a nursery rhyme.
A writer wondering what to write.

whose names

What should I write next?
A novel or a novella?
What topic do I wish to explore?

were Sunny and Rainy.

An owl at the door for sentinel stood.
And a merry old soul was he.
Who'll carry him to the grave?

My wife and I used to make this journey. About two or three times a week. It gives our son and his wife a break on the driving chores.

Yes sir yes sir – three bags full.

Finishing up a new novella. Wondering what my next writing-project is going to be. I always bring pens and paper. Once in a while, I pull over and jot down a sentence or two.

He was born as a mythical creature.

Driving to day-care to pick up my granddaughter.
Thinking about the books I'd like to write.

It gives me a break - a sufferer from such a disease - keeps us together - brainstorm for a bit - a few more snags - continued to chase each other - the credits roll by - which is which - lived in the dark - i am the victim.

*Mandfather Mouse
was feeling sad.
Through all his life
he had felt quite glad.*

Driving on to Elfrida. New houses encroaching on country fields. My granddaughter sings a nursery-song as we drive.

One for my master and one for my dame.

My wife used to read the nursery-books to our granddaughter. No doubt her parents do as well. And Tammie, the day-care lady, does the same. Together, they've covered just about every fairy-tale. For kids, the nursery-rhymes are in the air.

*The Sun was a very moody fellow.
He went from happiness to gloom and back again.
He had shone every day for many centuries.
He felt as if he would shine till the end of time.*

*It was just a drop of water.
Just one tiny drop
Amid the torrent
Of a raging mountain stream.
The drop considered its future
As it flowed.*

Mother Goose was probably born a human.

*Z was a Zany who looked a great fool.
They say the balloon is gone up to the moon.
And may not man, nor bird, nor beast this happy pair divide.*

I always bring milk and crackers. My granddaughter sings as we ride along. There's a crust of snow on the fields but the roads are bare and dry. Late February now, so spring will soon arrive.

And one for the little boy who lives down the lane.

Who was it who said there is only one story? – one human story – and that is all? That every life is an added chapter – and that every book is shining a light on a single tale? Perhaps no one said it – perhaps it was me.

A boy was born as a Human.

Enjoying the country landscape.
Enjoying my granddaughter singing a nursery rhyme.

Plunge back into the stream - looks like grass - there wasn't a crime - nor would anyone know - sip the bitter champagne - thankful for a respite - the week-end totals - set that thought aside - see what appeals to me - woke up from their curses.

*Aanteatipus Aardvark's life
had always been quite pleasant,
Although he dined on ants
rather than on pheasant.*

Today it's 'Ba Ba Black Sheep'. The other day it was 'Farmer in the Dell'. She knows 'Rain Rain Go Away' and all the other songs. She always sings a song as the miles go by.
Ba ba black sheep have you any wool?
Every human is living a story. We are born into fairy-tale kingdoms – variations on similar tales. Myths are the building-blocks of our grey-matter and our bones.

There were two celestial children

*A little girl choosing a toy.
A man sipping a coffee.
A drive through the countryside.*

whose names

What's the appeal of the nursery rhymes?
Why are they so enduring?
Do they go all the way back to the beginning of time?

were Rainy and Sunny.

Washroom, coffee, toy-store. A stop for her and a stop for me. She sips her milk and chews on her cracker. We always buy a little toy. Amazing what you can buy for seventy-five cents. It will keep her occupied as she sings her way home.

Yes sir yes sir – three bags full.

We are characters in *Crime and Punishment*. We are characters in *Wuthering Heights*. We are King Lear and Willie Loman and Oedipus too. Phaedra, Nora, Cleopatra – and on and on and on. We are the heirs of all the stories we make our own. In us every fairy-tale is rediscovered and renewed. We're as unique as our DNA allows us to be.

Chapter 2

It's just a bare stage. I'm one of a small crowd. Ten or fifteen of us at most, as I look around. A tent with washed-out canvas. 'Jack and the Beanstalk' in faded paint on a weathered marquee. The curtain parts and a boy comes out and bows. This is Jack – of Jack and the Beanstalk. He opens his hand and shows us some seeds. I join in when there's a smattering of applause.

Jack was a boy who lived with his widowed mother.

This is amazing. I'm feeling stunned. This is a carnival – a midway. In the midst of a farmer's field. Just like there used to be when I was a boy. I wonder where I am – and what brought me here. I don't think these people notice me – it's a very skimpy crowd. A series of tents with rickety stages arranged in a row.

Sunny and Rainy

A carnival in a farm field.
A story that would make a good film.
Water rushing through a canyon.

would chase each other

Have I traveled back in time?
Why does no human say hello?
Do carnivals still set up in farmers' fields?

around in the sky.

The snorting beast began to trot which galled him in his seat.
And when the weeds begin to grow it's like a garden full of snow.
She whipped him, she slashed him, she rode him through the mire.

It was an old clock that the owner had purchased at a flea market.
He was on his way to sell his mother's cow.

A man approaches – or is it a boy? An actor? – a mythical creature? – or one of the human crowd? Is this a costume? – or is he wearing regular clothes? John, he says – your name is John. Don't ask me how I know. I know who you are and I know why you are here. This is the Mother Goose Carnival of Tales. Mother Goose is around here somewhere. I'll explain things as we go. I'm Jack – of Jack and Jill fame. I'm the one who goes up the hill – to fetch a pail of water, as you probably know. Let's stroll along the midway. Mother Goose knows you're coming – she has a task for you. She'll tell you everything she wants you to know.

He spent his life in a nursery rhyme.

Finding myself at a carnival of fairy-tales.
Meeting Jack, of Jack and Jill fairy-tale fame.

My grandmother is a wolf! She has large teeth and she has glaring yellow eyes! She sits in a rocking chair and glares at me!

Encroaching on country fields - it comes alive - a failure to solve - stuck in this role - feel more connected - still on the circuit - acknowledging my feat - rescue of the baby - very thick o' hearing - the bucket was full of holes.

An old woman was sweeping her house,
and she found a little crooked sixpence.
"What," said she, "shall I do with this little sixpence?
I will go to market, and buy a little pig."

The moving-men
were coming today.
To take Mandfather Mouse's
furniture away.

We walk along the midway. Jack is showing me around. A nursery rhyme is being performed on every stage. We pause as we are talking. We stop in front of a tent. 'Little Miss Muffet' is painted on a marquee, in letters that are faded and worn. Only seven or eight have stopped to watch the play. A stage hand brings out a tuffet and sets it down at centre stage. A little boy in the audience starts to applaud and then he stops. The curtain parts and out comes a little girl. It's Little Miss Muffet holding a bowl of curds and whey. The little boy and his grandmother lead the applause.
Little Miss Muffet sat on a tuffet.
We are a carnival of tales, John, Jack is telling me. Mother Goose is the one in charge. She's the one who holds the gate-key – all we do here is perform – we don't make any decisions on our own. I'd like to talk when you get a

moment – though not in the presence of Mother Goose. I'm Jack – of Jack and Jill fame – please remember who I am – not Jack-be-Nimble or Jack-and-the-Beanstalk or any of those. I understand that you're a writer – I have something that I'd like to share with you.

The Sun was feeling deeply troubled.
My rays cause everything to grow.
I shine my rays in all directions
And everywhere a seed begins to stir.

My grandmother asks me to come closer! She says she wishes to tell me a tale! I am leery of the large teeth and the yellow eyes!

It had been a tiny ice-crystal
Locked shoulder to shoulder
Inside a glacier
For many thousands of years.
I felt just like a mummy
In a tomb.

She started out in life like everyone else.

R was a Robber who prowled about town.
The mischievous raven flew laughing away.
Little boy, pretty boy, where were you born?

As far as the clock knew, the time was centuries ago.
Eating her curds and whey.
Strolling with Jack along the midway. A little old lady approaches. Does she have a familiar face? – Old Mother Hubbard, perhaps – or the one who lives in a shoe? I am about to turn to Jack and ask who she can be. It's John! – I'd know you anywhere! – I think of you as a son! Come give your old Mother Goose a cheerful hug! I've been waiting for you, John! I want to introduce you to my brood! I've been looking around the midway! – something told me that you were here! I didn't know the day, but I knew the time! I just couldn't seem to pinpoint where you were! And now, I turn the corner and here you are!

He spent his life in a human world.

Strolling along the midway and watching the performances.
Surprised that such a carnival exists.

My grandmother tells me that I am not a foundling! I am not a baby lamb after all! She is my actual grandmother and I, too, am a wolf!

No one said it - a pack of wolves - make another list - can i trust you - see themselves in me - hate to disillusion her - whatever unknown means - plenty of gravitas - complexity and detail - take only what we need.

As she was coming home,
she came to a stile:
the piggy would not go over the stile.

Ants, to Aanteatipus Aardvark,
were quite delicious
And a bonus was that – he assumed –
they were quite nutritious.

We are strolling along the midway. Mother Goose is in the middle – Jack and I on either side. We pause, the three of us, at another stage. Every stage along the midway is about the same size. All the tents behind them are equally-faded too. About twenty-five people have stopped to watch Bo Peep. The curtain parts and a hand pushes a lamb out onto the stage. A pause and the lamb is followed by three bleating sheep. A shepherd's crook parts the curtain and through the opening steps Little Bo Peep. I'm relieved to hear the enthusiastic applause.

Little Bo Peep has lost her sheep.

I'm a little old for fairy-tales, but I remember them from my youth. I'd have known you anywhere, Mother Goose, though Jack I wouldn't have known. Now was it the beanstalk or the candlestick? – boys named 'Jack', I recall, seem to people the fairy-tales. I have three wonderful grandchildren – perhaps you already know. They grow up singing nursery rhymes – they learn them at home and at school. I didn't know there was a carnival – this whole scene is a big surprise. It reminds me of the days when I was a boy. The farmer's field – the tents – the stages – the curious crowds. These stories, I'm sure, go back through eons of time. I don't know how I got here, but there are some questions I'd like to ask, if you don't mind.

Rainy and Sunny

Daffodils peeking through the ground.
A Godmother trying to read blurry words.
A person sneaking through a fence.

would chase each other

How did Jack know my name?
And why did he say that Mother Goose was expecting me?

And why does she want to introduce me to her brood?

around in the sky.

The time that the clock announced was ancient, but the owner was never to know.
And doesn't know where to find them.
It's almost time for Jack's performance, so that leaves Mother Goose and I. We continue along the midway – a small crowd at every stage. The humans don't seem to see us – only the characters see Mother Goose and say hello. Jack said he had something to tell me – I wonder how long I'll get to be here – I assume I'll get to talk with him again. I can't see anything but farm-fields. Cars in a parking lot? – none I can see. Is the clothing from different eras? – different centuries, it seems to me. People don't seem to notice one another – it's for sure they don't notice me. It's as if I've gone back and I'm having a childhood dream.

Chapter 3

I'm an independent woman, John – a sculptor – in the story that I want you to write. I make marble statues – which I sculpt. Here let me show you what I mean. I'm talking to Jill – of Jack-and-Jill fame. We are together in the character-tent – after the show – and she is showing me a scene as we sit and talk. Jack tells me that you are a writer, John – you're exactly the person I need – though Jack need not hear of this 'til he hears it from me. Here I am on top of the quarry, John – the marble quarry at Carrera ... The coffee that Jill has provided turns out to be bitter – bitter and cold. Italy? – John? – you've heard of it? – the home of Carerra Marble? – the same that Michelangelo used to use? Here I am drilling the holes for the dynamite charge. I do all my own work, you see – from the quarry – to the sculpting – to the opening-night presentation of the work of art. Oh look – here I am plunging the plunger – see the dynamite explode? – see the block of marble sliding down the hill? I'm a young and successful sculptor, John – a female – on my own – world-renowned.

Jack and Jill went up the hill.

Oh – and here's a flashback – you don't mind flashbacks, do you, John? – I'm not aware of what kind of books you write. There's a car parked in the parking lot – see my marble sliding down? – in a moment, you will see the car squashed flat. And in it there's a lunch-box with some sandwiches and a thermos of coffee and beside it – on the seat – is what looks like a recipe-book. And the car and the thermos of coffee – and the sandwiches, of course – and the recipe-book as well – belong, you see, to Jack.

To fetch a pail of water.

We are gathered in the character-tent. I stand by Mother Goose's side. She wants to introduce me to the troupe. The tent is filled with familiar faces – drawn from dozens of nursery-rhymes – Jack, from Jack Sprat Could Eat No Fat – Jack, from Jack and Jill Went up the Hill – Jack, from Jack Be Nimble Jack Be Quick. They sit on the chairs and spill out into the midway. It's morning, so none of the human crowd has arrived. Mother Goose shushes for quiet and then she speaks. Now John is a famous detective! – you might have read some of his books! I have always thought of John as somewhat of a son! The characters look at me and at Mother Goose and back again. John has graciously come at my bidding! – says Mother Goose to the troupe – to help me solve what I'm sure has been a crime! Now, I don't want to cause alarm! – oh no – but it's very clear to me that some of our characters go missing almost every day! You are aware of the empty stages! – I can see some of the signs from here! John is going to conduct some interviews! – he'll be talking with all of you! Please give him your full cooperation! – as if you were talking to me! John has cracked some very big cases! – he runs ahead of the fastest bloodhounds! – he is more devious than the most devious-minded of crooks! Criminals tremble when John approaches! – they know they'll soon be locked in prison! – and reading about themselves in one of his books!

When Sunny was close to the Earth,

A girl telling the story of her dreams.
Produce placed on an altar.
Two celestial children playing a game.

the Earth

What's all this about a crime?
What other writer does she have in mind?
What makes her think that I write detective-books?

would be bathed in sunshine.

His goose had laid him an egg of pure gold.
Six precious souls, and all agog to dash through thick and thin.
If we ventured down this morning, you would eat us up, I fear.

Let's walk around, John – says Mother Goose – and watch some shows on the midway and I'll introduce you to some of the performers. They'll all be willing to talk with you – they're a very friendly lot. The faded sign says 'Jack and Jill Went up the Hill'. Three stage hands come out on the stage. One stage hand places a wooden bucket at one side of the stage and the other two place a well on the other side. Perhaps there's something they might have heard, John – maybe something has caught their eye. I'm sure, John, that with your experience – I am always amazed when I think of your books – something small – something tiny – something infinitesimal – might well turn out to be a massive clue. Jack comes out on the stage, lifts up the wooden bucket and turns it upside down. Jill comes out on the stage and Jack shows the upside-down bucket to Jill and then points to the well across the stage.
Jack fell down and broke his crown.
Duquaquious Duck lived in a dry pond on the side of a hill.

He spent all his time with other mythical creatures.

Meeting the fairy-tale characters in the morning.
Surprised by the speech that Mother Goose makes.

This was going to be a ballad
To be called 'The Mother Goose Crime'
But such a title is not yet valid
As out of joint, it seems, is the time.

We are characters - hasn't acknowledged a word - warmth has passed - cut
the lifeline - do some thinking - hen in a storm - two celestial children - all my
yearnings - knew all the nursery rhymes - certainly not going to happen.

She went a little farther,
and she met a dog.
So she said to the dog —
"Dog, dog, bite pig;
Piggy won't get over the stile;
And I shan't get home to-night."
But the dog would not.

All of Mandfather Mouse's
friends and family were gone.
It was time for Mandfather Mouse
to move on.

So here I am in my studio, John. Jill is showing me a scene. The other
fairy-tale characters sit and chat in the character-tent. The summer night is
warn and there's a moon. This would be – if you are counting – the second
scene. Surrounding me – in my studio – in a loft in mid-Manhattan ... I sip my
cold, bitter coffee as we sit and watch the scene. In New York, John? – it's a
borough? – I assumed that you would know. Surrounding me – as I was saying
– there are busts, cast in clay – but your readers can't tell yet, because each
one – each bust – is covered by a cloth. I am working on a new one, John – for
a commission that I have received. I went to boarding-school with a girl from
a tiny country – at the furthest end of the map. A revolution when she returns
– her father is President for Life – he wants his face to be on a mountain – just
like the Rushmore-presidents are – and his daughter persuades him to give the
commission to me. So I am making a model, John – from a photograph of my
best friend's father. See the jewels that encrust his uniform? – see me modelling them with my hands in the squishy clay? I am working as your readers
absorb the scene. But then – I stop my modelling, John! – I throw my scalpel
down! – I lurch around the room! – insanely, John, I am tearing off the cloths!

Then we – your readers, John – see all the models in one wide scene. Every model that I have modelled has the face of – Jack!

Up Jack got, and home did trot.

Oh, and there's a flashback here as well, John – of Jack and I in court – he is suing me for squashing – with my marble block – his car. He was parked in a restricted zone – I was blasting in a restricted zone, above – neither one of us was aware that we were breaking the law. The judge sneers that we make a good pair – that we're 'two of a kind'– 'birds of a feather' – that for two cents he'd lock us up together and swallow the key. We hear – the readers, hear, John – and see the blast again. Jack is running towards the car – a piece of marble dents his safety-helmet – Jack loses a part of his memory. His mother used to make his sandwiches – but she has passed away – he's used her recipe every lunch-time since she has died. Now his mind has holes like cheese, John – Swiss, I am sure you will write – and the recipe-book for the sandwiches was squashed in the car.

As fast as he could caper.

Jack and Jill mime climbing the hill as they move across the stage. The climb is so strenuous for both of them – as their faces show – that I strain my muscles involuntarily to try to help. When they reach the well, Jack puts the bucket in and – with straining muscles – draws the full, wooden bucket back out. We winter in Sarasota, John, continues Mother Goose – did you know it's a circus town? We pitch our tents and lick our wounds and attempt to regroup. We move north and tour the country when comes the spring. The troupe is a little smaller now, John – we have fallen on difficult times. There isn't a nursery-story I haven't toured in my prime. I've been a fan of yours for ages – somehow I'm drawn to the mystery genre. I wanted a writer – a mystery-writer – one with a backlog of cases solved. No matter how tough the conundrum, you always come through – you have a mind that snarls at crime and takes a big bite. I hope I'm not keeping you from your writing. Did you wonder, John, how I managed to summon you here?

When I was young, thought the Sun,
I saw myself as a cleansing agent.
I assumed I would wash all negatives down the drain.
That I would be a new broom to sweep things clean.

There are two writers in this story.
One writer is present and one is not.
Perhaps the crime-scene will be gory.
One is a sleuth and one is not.

Global warming had set it free
And now the tiny drop of water
Raced eagerly down the mountainside.

I wonder where I'll live.
I wonder what I'll do.
I have many years of life
Ahead of me.

She raised geese and sold them at country fairs.

And the thick mud has covered his legs and his feet.
If it be to-morrow day, take your wings and fly away.
Three straws on a staff would make a baby cry and laugh.

On the way down the steep hill, Jack suddenly slips, and the wooden buck-et rolls across the stage. Jack tumbles over and over as if he is falling down. Immediately, Jill slips on the steep slope and comes tumbling after. I'm think-ing – John – of murder – Mother Goose confides to me – or of kid-napping, at least. I made a list in Sarasota – we winter there, as you know. All the acts that were part of the troupe – all the characters who were with us when we took to the road. I can't seem to find that list – John – perhaps it has been purloined. I want you to find the culprit, John – a conspiracy, do you think? What would you say is causing the shortage of nursery-rhymes? Mother Goose looks me squarely in the eye. The assignment, John – the task – the requirement – the need – is to find out whether there has been a crime committed – who has been murdered or kid-napped – when this crime occurred, and – if a crime has been committed – who is guilty. This is the task, John, and nothing short of that. She assures me – as we watch the two characters tumbling – that she will introduce me to Jill later on.
He went to bed to mend his head.
If only I could invent a way for water to flow uphill thought Duquaquious Duck.

He spent all his time with other humans.

Meeting Jill at the character-tent after the performance.
Hearing the story that Jill would like to be in.

A Fairy Godmother is vexed.
She is engaged in a frantic search.
If she cannot find her specs
A reputation will be besmirched.

Opens his hand - all the major historians - sunlight broke through - i wouldn't know - snow will melt away - end of his rope - carry him to the grave - wouldn't complain or sue - all there in the fairy-stories - picked themselves up.

She went a little farther,
and she met a stick.
So she said—
"Stick, stick, beat dog;
Dog won't bite pig;
Piggy won't get over the stile,
And I shan't get home to-night."
But the stick would not.

But one day, Aanteatipus Aardvark
saw two ants walking together
And he wondered whether they
were a daughter and a mother.

So here I am on Mount Rushmore, John. You know that mountain, I assume. It's much more famous than Italy or Manhattan, so you must have heard. Jill and I find ourselves in the scene – the Presidents are an awe-inspiring sight. I am here doing research, John – Scene Three, if you're keeping count. I want the head of my best friend's father – the head of the President for Life – to rival the four American presidents in prestige. Suddenly, John, I slip! – see me tumbling? – see me fall? I am dangling by a rope from the end of a nose! The rope is beginning to fray, John! – I hold it in my hands! – in hopes that someone will reach out a hand and rescue me!

With vinegar and brown paper.

Oh – and another flashback here, John. Jack and I don't get along – he has to hitchhike to work, you see – at the quarry – and with the loss of the recipe-book – and his memory – remember the cheese? – he doesn't enjoy his lunches – at work – at all. But just before I left, John – on my Rushmore research-trip – I found a lunch-box just like the one he used to leave in the parking lot – in what used to be his car – and I made some sandwiches, John – like my mother used to make – and some coffee with my own special blend – and sent it to him, John, with a tender note. So moved is he by the sandwiches, John – I always start with a slice of cheese – by coincidence, it's Swiss – who would believe? – and lettuce – Raddichio lettuce – which not everyone would use – but especially by the coffee – so close, in taste – who would know? – to what his mother used to make – I'm always precise, John, when I count the pieces of shell – that he has followed me to Mount Rushmore – see him emerge from a tourist bus? – at the moment when I am dangling from the rapidly-fraying rope.

Jack and Jill went up the hill.

Or should it be Jack – do you think? – I'm an independent female – who is dangling from the nose and fears to fall? Perhaps Jack should be the sculptor – no, that wouldn't work at all. Well – maybe the brakes on the tourist bus fail – and I rescue him somehow – I would still be measuring the nose, but I wouldn't fall. I see the tourist bus in the distance – I have a sense of impending disaster – surely the brakes on the bus are faulty – my ears insist there's something wrong when I hear them squeal.

To fetch a pail of water.

Well, that is my story John – I have an ending in mind, of course. So – what do you think – when you write this – will happen to us, John? – to Jack and Jill in our no-longer-children roles? Shall I get you another coffee? – finish your drink and I'll get you some more. It's time for us to move on, John – I've given Jack a substantial role – from the eight-line snippet of Jack breaking his crown. I'm so sure, John, that our audience will agree. Let it cool before you swallow – it's always too hot, I find – though the recipe for the blend they got from me. I haven't told Jack yet – perhaps you can tell him – show him your writing – be my advocate – make my case. He must have sensed that I'm growing restless – my tumbling isn't what it was. I get so tired of enacting the tumbling-after fall.

Jack fell down and broke his crown.

I'm sorry to hear about all your troubles, Mother Goose. I'd like to apologize. I've known about you since I was a little boy. However, I've been insensitive. I've had a one-dimensional mind. I've never thought of you as composed of more than your public persona. Life – for you – has been quite difficult and I have been totally unaware. All this time you've been struggling – a swimmer calling for aid – while I have been making sand-castles – and didn't know.

When Rainy was close to the Earth,

A border that Humans cannot cross.
Sailors lacking confidence in their leader.
A baby suspended in the air.

the Earth

Am I an actor in a drama?
If so, should I just play along?
And am I free, then, to improvise my role?

would be bathed in rain.

My wife and I were in Sarasota – though it was many years ago. We toured the Circus World in the winter time. Elephants and lions and tigers – tight-rope-walkers and acrobats – but there was nothing about Mother Goose and her nursery rhymes. Should I tell her that I have been there? – don't want to accuse her of telling a lie. And why does she say that I'm a detective? – a detective who also writes books? And how do I tell her that I don't have a clue about solving her crimes?

And Jill came tumbling after.

If I were a beaver, I would know a lot more about the properties of water, thought Duquaquious Duck.

Chapter 4

Oh yes, I want children, John – lots and lots of children – in the story I want you to write – but not my own this time. I want to mother every child in the whole wide world. I am talking with the little old lady who lives in a shoe. Her eyes are as lively as they must have been when she was a girl. She is telling me of the person she longs to be. Here is what I want you to write, John – I've been told you write lots of books – I'm sure you'll agree that the plot will be perfect for me. Let me be born in a war-torn country, John. Here I am in my ballet class. Hear the bombs as they drop, John? – hear the explosions from time to time? Each time the destruction is nearer to the hall. I am always very thin, John – never having enough to eat. Hear the other girls jeering at me, John? – make them cruel – nasty – unkind. They think my legs are too thin to carry me through the grind of ballet – that they'll snap right off whenever I make a leap. But I have something going for me, John – something none of the other girls have. My toes have a wider span than the average child of my age – even a child, unlike me, who is getting enough to eat. Have you ever heard of Nijinski, John? – did you ever practice ballet? – his toes are splayed so wide that he can make gigantic leaps. But I must never look like a freak, John – when you describe me, keep this in mind – always make me look as fragile as a swan. But I shall leap to balletic heights, John – higher than any other girl. Only Nijinski is known to leap higher – though he is a boy. I become a major star, John, as the bombs rain down from above – opening nights – standing ovations – lush bouquets. But the bombs are always present, John – the bombs rain down as I practice my pliés.

There was an old woman who lived in a shoe.

Jack and I stroll along the midway. The faded sign says 'There Was an Old Lady Who Lived in a Shoe'. Look, John – let me give you the lowdown, Jack is telling me. There never was a list. Or if there was – if she found it – or you found it for her – it wouldn't reveal a thing. Mother Goose has a mind like a punctured sieve. Every year, when she sets out from Sarasota – as soon as winter breaks and spring is on the way – she attempts to make a list – to get the whole thing organized – but it doesn't happen. Two stage hands come out on stage and pull the curtains back as wide as they can go. A large shoe begins to emerge from backstage. The shoe catches on the curtains and the stage hands tug at the curtains as the shoe is being pushed from behind.

When Rainy was close to the Earth,

A faded sign above a stage on a midway.
Humans believing in the power of prayer.
A few seeds in an open hand.

the Earth

What does Jack mean by 'the lowdown'?
Why would it matter if there was no list?
How could this information help to solve the crime?

would be bathed in rain.

Looking as happy as happy could be.
I'll tell you a story about John-a-Nory.
Nay, I'll not give my fiddle to any man alive.

All things are true at all times, said Heraclitus, or one of those other Greek philosophers in the agora.
She had so many children she didn't know what to do.
Suddenly, ten or a dozen raggedly-dressed children pour out through a door in the toe of the shoe. Some skip rope, some play hopscotch, and others kneel down and play at marbles. Though the small crowd is quiet, the children on the stage make a lot of noise. But it isn't entirely Mother Goose's fault, Jack continues explaining to me. These Mythicals are like kids, John – a bunch of unruly kids. It's embarrassing for me to think of myself as one. Some leave before she's ready – say they'll meet her along the way. Others stay behind – their presentation isn't quite right – just a few more snags to untangle and they'll be sure to follow along. Others show up on the road – can you put me on the stage? Others wander off in the night and disappear.

One of his friends was always tumbling down a hill.

Strolling with Jack along the midway.
Wondering why he is so eager to talk to me.

We are walking in the woods! Two babes completely lost! It is dark and we are cold! Our wicked stepmother has turned us out in the blustery snow!

A little crooked sixpence - not being noticed or praised at all - the sponge is dry - hold the world together - wondering what to write - a single candle's glow - looked a great fool - on top of the quarry - washed-out canvas - hard to take.

> *She went a little farther,*
> *and she met a fire.*
> *So she said—*
> *"Fire, fire, burn stick;*
> *Stick won't beat dog;*
> *Dog won't bite pig;*
> *Piggy won't get over the stile;*
> *And I shan't get home to-night."*
> *But the fire would not.*

> *Mandfather Mouse lived*
> *in a wall in a house.*
> *It had been a good life*
> *for this aging mouse.*

Now here's my second scene, John. This is what you can make me be. It's the old lady who lives in a shoe – she is telling me of the person she wishes to be. It's shortly after the war, of course. I'm a movie star in the pictures, John – I play light romantic roles – the prince always marries me in the end. The ballet stage is my launching-pad, John – Hollywood comes and whisks me away. I star in a series of films that are highly-acclaimed – in one I play a ballet-girl during a war. I sign autographs – I have fan-clubs – my face is on marquees all over the world. All the material comforts are left, overnight, at my door. But I am a person of great sadness, John – a lady of sorrows galore. If you notice, John – I can't hide it – it's written all over my face. Even the way I kiss the prince seems to give it away. It's guilt, John – guilt – though I have personally done no wrong. It's that my fortunes have soared so high, John – as high as Nijinski, one critic will say – while those other girls – you recall them, John? – the ones who sneered as I practiced ballet? – are wallowing in poverty and pain. The thought of them – of their suffering – makes me yearn to set things right. Oh yes– I live in a mansion, John – after all I'm a movie star – I'd have nowhere else to live if I didn't live there. Acres of blooming orchids, John – vivid flamingoes arrayed in the yard. See the splendid staircase reaching to the stars? But my thoughts, John – see my eyes? – as I sip the bitter champagne? – as my maid arranges the orchids by the pool? – go back, you see – far back – to my childhood, war-torn days. Bombs rain down on me in my mansion, John – on the mansion-lawn of my mind. You can write about the explosions that I still hear. The maid removes my slippers, John – my toes resume their splay – I can never forget the girl that I used to be.
She gave them some broth without any bread.

A little old lady emerges from the door in the toe of the shoe. She calls out to the children for quiet, but they ignore her and continue playing their noisy games. The old lady throws her hands up in the air in exasperation. We are myths – John – myths, Jack explains. We only exist in the public mind. If fewer and fewer people think about us, as time goes by, we tend to fade. Things have changed in recent times, John – there's been harshness to endure. The crowds are thinner – the costumes are threadbare – our relevance fades with the sun and the rain. Patches are holding the fabric together, if you know what I mean. Performers don't always take it in stride, John. We set up all over the country – despair can strike at any time – some will just jump across a ditch and disappear.

But I realized, in time, to my horror,
Thought the Sun,
That I cause all things to happen.
Every seed takes inspiration from my womb.

A large woodsman appears on the trail! It is dark but his axe-blade gleams! He moves towards us rapidly and we turn and flee!

The torrent rushed along a canyon.
The little drop was carried along.
It dodged the jagged rocks of the mountainside.
Not one other drop of water ever spoke to him.
I am sure that we are equally occupied.

The sides of the canyon were steep.
All the water stayed inside.
The little drop thought of his future.
Perhaps I will power industry
Or raise a single plant in a pot.
He wondered what his future was going to be.

One day, she had an idea that made her a Mythical.

If I had half-a-crown a day I'd spend it all upon you.
And come with a good will, or not at all.
And they played together kindly in the dark pine-tree.

Not all things are true at all times, said Heraclitus's brother, or perhaps a friend, in the agora. Some things are true at all times and other things are not.
Then whipped them all soundly and sent them to bed.
I watch as the little old lady tries in vain to catch the attention of her many children. But sometimes a miracle can happen, John, Jack continues telling

me. Something that catches the mood of the day – and then the crowds swell on the midway – demand for tickets will suddenly soar – and a myth will be the flavour of the day. You are a writer, John – a writer. Perhaps you should ask yourself just why you are here today. Mother Goose's troubles aside, John, I sense that you are troubled too. We Mythicals are super-sensitive, you know. In fact, I sense something, John, about you. You are a writer, John, for sure – however, I am getting a clear sensation – and these sensations of mine are seldom proven wrong. I tend to zero in on the essence of each concern. It's a sensation, John, that you are a writer – who finds it hard – extremely hard – to come up with ideas. But not everyone is so conception-impoverished where inspiration is concerned. Fate has brought us together – I'm sure of it, John – I feel more connected to you than I've ever felt to Jill. I'm sure I can help you, John, by giving you some ideas – ideas that – together – we can turn into a new story – John – for me. The performance comes to an end and the little old lady and the children all link hands and bow, to a smattering of enthusiastic applause. The stage hands come out to remove the shoe as Jack and I move on.

There was an old woman who lived in a shoe.

It wouldn't happen with me, John, says Jack, as we stroll along the midway. I'd either have wider curtains or a smaller shoe.

One of his friends was always collecting garbage.

Watching the lady who lives in the shoe give her performance.
Meeting her afterwards for a chat in the character-tent.

The large woodsman catches us! He tells us that we are actually his children! That the wicked stepmother stole us away at birth!

Garden full of snow - so let's get started - all items fit inside - made the people laugh - only think of themselves - an unlit candlestick - born as a human - willing to talk with you - why you are here - stories with darker moods.

She went a little farther,
and she met some water.
So she said —
"Water, water, quench fire;
Fire won't burn stick;
Stick won't beat dog;
Dog won't bite pig;
Piggy won't get over the stile;
And I shan't get home to-night."
But the water would not.

If an ant were hurrying home

to its family
Being eaten would be
an Aanteatipus-made catastrophe.

The old lady who lives in a shoe continues her story. It's a story that she would like me to place her in. I won't be happy living in a mansion, John – any more than I was in the shoe. I'll keep searching for my rightful place in the world. I'm not interested in personal glory – when you write this you can skip the many awards and accolades. I would confine all that to merely a chapter or two – just to indicate – in retrospect – the enormous sacrifice that later – after much brooding beside my swimming pool – I give my head a shake and decide to make. Here I am in my later years, John – what I want you to have me be. I have many children now – see them pressing forward to greet me – so lovingly – as I descend – with appropriate music – from on high – towards the runway – towards the ground? No more living in a shoe, John – I have my own private plane. The fuselage gleams on the tarmac – strewn with petals from many lands – bouquets of splendid orchids fill my arms. Oh they're not my personal children – no – they are the waifs from war-torn lands. I bring them food and comfort, John – I see their plight as my own. A Mother-Teresa figure, for sure, John – in how I am blessed with the common touch – we both of us are so gifted at molding young lives. The children greet me on the runway – I pose for pictures with groups of them, John. I have a cameraman follow me constantly – yes, the world must know my pain. I am still – in my mind and heart, John – that skinny, war-torn waif – rejected and scorned at ballet-school. The Swan-lake chorus was needlessly cruel, John – they hid the special socks I had made – swans-down feathers concealing adders or reptiles of some other odious kind. Oh those memories burn like sulphur, John – torture-chambers, they are, in my mind. I hear the bombs rain down incessantly, John – I am still that humble child. I am atoning for others' crimes, John – leaving my mansion for weeks at a time. I want those children, John, to see themselves in me. I show them my splayed toes, John – my splayed Nijinski-toes – the ugly duckling who leapt so high she became a swan. I'm leaping higher than ever before, John. Have me leaping. John, when you write this. Show a little girl who is suffering – take the reader inside her thoughts. Have me leaping – John – inside that little girl's heart.

She had so many children she didn't know what to do.

I'm certainly flattered by your offer, Jack. How kind of you to want to help me out. But I assure you that I am not now – and never have been – a sufferer from such a disease as writer's block. I have a dozen projects waiting outside my door. They squeeze themselves in and make a pitch whenever I open the door a crack – to fetch the newspaper or go out for a breath of air. But if you don't mind my asking, Jack – I'm sure you'll be candid with me – how did you know that I was a writer? – and what makes you think that I am in need of aid?

When Sunny was close to the Earth,

A cow whose feat is unrecognized.
A sense of dark and sinister forces.
Wildebeests drinking their fill.

the Earth

Why would Jack want me to write a story for him?
Would this mean that he would leave the carnival?
Would it mean he'd no longer act in his nursery rhyme?

would be bathed in sunshine.

It is the task of everyone at all times to know which is which at any time, said either Heraclitus or another brother, or another friend, in the agora that day.

She gave them some broth without any bread.

I don't really care for Jack – there's something about this whole situation that isn't quite right. Jack says he intends to tell me a story – Jill tells me one as well. So – stay calm – John – and do some thinking. Thinking has always been your forté. Now – the topic is never the topic – this is an adage that I firmly believe. So – I'll look beneath the surface – and see what I can see. Whose idea was it to bring me here – by whatever unknown means it has been achieved? The answer will be – it seems to me – the needed – the essential – clue.

Then whipped them all soundly and sent them to bed.

No, I don't run ahead of the bloodhounds, but I can sense the smell of red herring as I pause – for a moment and sniff – with discernment – the air, while keeping my eye on the true – the actual – the Jack-built – mystery, that only I – apparently – alone – am able – it seems – to see. Surface-logic says that it was Mother Goose – to save her enterprise. Most detectives would stop right there – gaze at the mountains and miss the borrows under their feet – but suppose – to take the less-travelled surmise – it just might be our boy, Jack – of Jack and Jill fame – whose motive just might be to escape from his present situation – his eternal situation – at the expense of Mother Goose and her enterprise. Now – assuming I'm on the right track – that I have sniffed, with my mind, the tell-tale spoor – if Jack were to take a role in another story – followed by Jill and the other characters – if they were to change their stories, too – the Mother Goose midway would be as empty as a ghost town – and there would be no more traditional nursery rhymes.

Chapter 5

I'll be born on the wrong side of town, John – in this story – so my tale will be pretty basic – brutal and blunt – when you write it for me. Little Boy Blue puts his horn on the table and settles down to tell me his yarn. There's a word you might not want to use, John – don't know how nasty you get in your books. You might want to call it – politely – 'a house of ill-repute' – to protect your reader's ears, John – but it's 'a whorehouse' in the lingo I'm using with you. I'm just a little boy, and one day a customer can't pay. There's a rumour that he's my father, but I wouldn't know. The thing that started the rumour, John, is my mother's favourite song – 'You are My Sunshine'. Night after night he's been trying to learn it, but it's just no go. So anyway, he has this sheepish look, as he tells the girls he's broke, but he says he'll leave his battered horn behind. There's a slight twitch – when he's nervous – beside his left eye. He says he's never been a great horn-player – maybe the kid could give it a try. He says there's a battered fiddle in the pawn shop – maybe he'll have some better luck if he saws the strings. He puts the old horn in my hands – there's that twitch in the eye again – and I press my face against the screen door and watch him go.

Little Boy Blue come blow your horn.

The faded sign says 'Little Boy Blue Come Blow Your Horn'. It all started with just an idea, John – Mother Goose is telling me – far, far back in the mists of ancient time. I was spending an afternoon at a country fair. I was there, John, to sell my surplus geese. After the sale, John, I decided to wander around. There was a lute player and an acrobat – each would entertain on a stage. Shade and sunshine – pleasant weather – the stage had been set up under a tree. I was standing in the audience – and I thought – all at once – of the world of the nursery rhyme. Myths are what holds the world together, John. They are written – they are told – we are acting them, John – at the level that unites all humankind. Take Jack and Jill for instance – who in the world has not climbed a hill, John – set out on a quest – to fetch whatever it was that they'd set their sights on? And who in the world has not fallen down, John – broken their crown and even worse – and not picked themselves up and climbed that hill again? Myths are stories that we tell about ourselves, John – about every human being – about every person in the world – every one. As we share them, we are all holding hands. Why not put them, John, on stage for all to see?

The Humans Beings who lived on the Earth

A boy telling a story to a man.
A girl working on a sculpture.
Mythical characters straggling along a road.

feared

So – myths are stories that we tell?
Stories we tell about ourselves?
Should I search for myself in every nursery rhyme?

the drought and desiccation of the sun.

Curl your locks as I do mine; two before and two behind.
She threw him down upon the ground which made the people laugh.
When it did bleed, then blood it did run.

Two stage hands come out on stage. One shakes out a green rug which looks like grass and places it on one side of the stage. The other stage hand carries a frame of fence-rails which holds corn-stalks and places the frame on the other side of the stage. I had to coax – John – adds Mother Goose – all these people – these mythical characters, you would say – to come out of the rhymes – out of the books and the songs – and present themselves on stage. People had never seen them in person, John – they had never been able to see these characters live. Well – more and more characters came to join me. We would travel from town to town. We built the stages and sewed the tents and painted the signs. Bigger towns – larger audiences – success like I didn't dare to dream. Every country around the world, John – long before airplanes or even big ships. Not a child who wouldn't come out to see nursery rhymes.
The sheep's in the meadow – the cow's in the corn.
Vice-admiral Alsevenseas Albatross was the vice-admiral of the Albatross Fleet.

Another friend was always jumping a candlestick.

Strolling along with Mother Goose in the midway.
Enjoying the plays as she tells me of her cares.

She squints her eyes and reads her diary.
Her eyesight steers her wrong.

The print she sees is blurry.
She casts a spell on a writer named John.

Know you anywhere - what else could it possibly be - every thought and every action - avoided it in my speech - come on all these rides - becoming a miserable chore - always sings a song - the squishy clay - i turn the corner - the one that got mangled.

She went a little farther,
and she met an ox.
So she said—
"Ox, ox, drink water;
Water won't quench fire;
Fire won't burn stick;
Stick won't beat dog;
Dog won't bite pig;
Piggy won't get over the stile;
And I shan't get home to-night."
But the ox would not.

Into a sack Mandfather Mouse
stuffed his clothes.
He threw the sack over his shoulder
and walked down the road.

Well that horn makes me a prodigy – John – I pick it up and it comes alive. I become the youngest horn-player to make the scene. Every joint from New York to Chicago – every dive from there to LA. Diamond rings on all my fingers – they catch the lights as I rear back and play – smoky rooms and late nights and wads and wads of dough. And no matter what goes down, John – bar-fights – police raids – broken pool cues on the floor – I end the gig with my mother's favourite song – 'You are My Sunshine'. But the whole scene begins to turn sour, John – dark forces lurk in the woodwork – shades of the whore-house lour over me – fiends snatch at me from Hell and drag me down. Drug addiction – do you know what that entails, John? – it's taking a needle and spritzing poison into your veins. Self-medication, John – an attempt to deaden the pain. I'm going nowhere – zip – downhill – only a coffin could bring the agony to heel. Then an auto accident occurs – I cut up my face and mangle my lip, John – see me crawling away from the wreck as she loudly explodes? Here I am in a hospital bed, John – see my arm bound up like a mummy? – there's a cable up to the ceiling and down again. The doctor is telling me that I'll never again play the horn. I'm feeling low, John – a friend brings some bourbon – I take a swig in my hospital bed. Delirium tremens, John – palm trees, blue skies, a bourbon-filled oasis. I dog-paddle, John – lapping feverishly – around the lagoon. If the bottle was bigger I'd dive inside and drown.

But where is the boy who looks after the sheep?

Troubles pile on troubles – a pyramid of woes – my bedclothes feel like quicksand – my misfortunes breed like flies. I develop a twitch, John – on my face – beside my left eye. My nostrils flinch at the stench of my sewer-like soul.

He's under the haystack fast asleep.

A stage hand comes on stage leading a sheep with a rope and a weight. The stagehand places the weight down on the carpet of grass and the sheep looks out at the audience. A second stage hand comes out leading a cow with a rope and a weight. He places the weight next to the stand of corn. The cow and the sheep stand on the stage and look at the audience. Now the crowds are smaller, John – continues Mother Goose – the tents are all faded, ripped and torn. It's getting hard to hold it together – it seems my characters come and go. They are like children, John, irresponsible children – they were spoiled in the early days. More popular than they could handle – you wouldn't believe the size of the crowds. Now they have to work for an audience – some of them find it hard to take – some of them get depressed at the meager size of the crowds. They just take off, John, and wander who knows where.

The seeds of aging and corruption –
The seeds of cruelty and of despair –
Thought the Sun, sadly –
All stir when they feel the warmth of my regard.

There is a man who is a detective.
He is also a man who writes books.
Are his Godmother's powers defective?
Are her purposes mistook?

A stream ran through a desert.
Many drops were drawn to the sky,
But the little drop moved forward
As the stream meandered on.
I'm being saved for something.
I wonder what it will be.

She saw the human need for folk-tales.

When the blazing sun is gone, when he nothing shines upon.
They found a bird's nest with five eggs in.
She brings us good tidings and tells us no lies.

Little Boy Blue comes out on stage. He acknowledges the smattering of applause with a slight smile. He moistens his lips and then he raises his horn and adjusts his pucker and begins to blow on the horn. I'd rather not talk of my fears, John, Mother Goose intones. I believe in a sinister force – always lurking outside the grounds – testing and probing for any weakness – a pack of wolves that watches the fold. I don't dwell upon this notion, John – I avoided it in my speech. It might affect their performance – art is not life, it is life refined – let them present the world as cheerful and happy and bright. But there's something in the air, John – something that doesn't like nursery rhymes – that insists on deeper stories with darker moods. Something is diminishing my tales, John – making them fewer, if you know what I mean. Killing them, John – if I force myself to be blunt. That is why I fear for the fate of the missing ones. Little Boy Blue is taking his bow to a smattering of applause, as two stage hands come out to clear the stage. Mother Goose tells me that she will introduce me to Little Boy Blue.

Will you wake him? – no, not I.

Vice-admiral Alsevenseas Albatross's sailors liked him – as an person – for sure – but didn't have much confidence in the readiness of his warships to engage in combat should the necessity ever occur.

One of his friends was always teaching school.

Meeting with Little Boy Blue in the character-tent.
Feeling surprised at the role he would like to play.

He is the world's greatest detective.
The world's greatest writer as well.
Is his Godmother's wand defective?
Has she misread her book of spells?

The opening steps - the way we live today - you live your life - complete with a basket - covered in ice today - that shouldn't matter - rushing through a canyon - many years of life - about the same size - rolling like a tsunami.

She went a little farther,
and she met a butcher.
So she said—
"Butcher, butcher, kill ox;
Ox won't drink water;
Water won't quench fire;
Fire won't burn stick;
Butcher will not kill ox;
Stick won't beat dog;
Dog won't bite pig;
Piggy won't get over the stile;

And I shan't get home to-night."
But the butcher would not.

His body grew thin as Aanteatipus Aardvark
continued to brood.
He would die if he didn't find
an alternative source of food.

But there's still another scene, John – I overcome all the odds. I have a comeback that nobody in the music business can believe. Here I am standing on stage – John – the Hollywood Bowl or Carnegie Hall – one of those cavernous, prestigious music venues. See me standing there all alone in the spotlight's glow? I moisten my lip – the battered lip – the one that got mangled when the car went smash – and then I raise the horn to my lips and try to blow. Well – it's never worked in rehearsal – I don't think I can do it, John – but they push me out on stage just the same. At least give it a try says my manager and gives me a shove. You'll hate yourself if you don't try it, says my mother – she's retired from the whorehouse by now. And there's other friends as well – all the hobos and the bums that I met when I was lying in those alleys with two or three needles sticking out of my arms. They're sitting with bated breath in the very first row. I'm standing there on stage, John – I know I can't play the horn. But then a miracle starts to happen – I see it walking across the stage. You guessed it – my father turns up out of nowhere just for this scene. His eye is twitching as he tells me that I am his son. I feel new life in my lip, John. He twitches and whispers again. He says he will marry my mother and make her legit – but only if I play her favourite song – 'You are My Sunshine'. Then he goes and sits beside her and they hold hands. I have what I call a transformation – a transcendence – a seismic shift – an epiphany, transposed – transcribed – arranged – for harp or horn. My eye is twitching madly, John – a butterfly dancing on red-hot coals. I raise the horn to my lips and then I blow. Well, you won't believe this, John – there won't be a dry eye among your readers – their tears will blur the pages of your book. The purest notes your readers have ever heard, John. Their eyes will look up to the ceiling – they won't believe these notes are coming from a human horn. Sure, there's no music in a novel, John, but I'm sure you can do it with words. You've got to make your readers believe they're hearing those notes – in my mind I see thousands of readers humming along. Little Boy Blue has told me his story. All the tents have been battened down – the nursery-rhyme characters sit and chat. It's a long way from the sheep in the meadow – the cows in the corn.

For if I do he's sure to cry.

And there could be a sequel, John. It's a saga, I'm sure you'll agree. Remember my father and the old battered fiddle? We'll get together and play duets – form a father-and-son duo and go out on the road. We'll work up an act for a Vegas performance – I replace Gabriel on the Day of Judgement – he develops a cyst on his throat – and my father spells off Nero on the day that Rome burns. One of those big extravaganzas that Vegas does so well – the special effects, John, you can describe as out of this world. Then the two of us go on tours all over the world, John – stadiums bursting and airports crazy with eager fans. We appear with symphony orchestras and teach them my mother's song. Father and son together – together like brothers – together like pals. We do commercials for horns and fiddles – it starts a world-wide musical craze. The money comes rolling in like a tsunami – a mile-high tide. We'll be the biggest stars of our time, John – bigger than kings – bigger than popes. We could spin this out forever – ever franchise any of your books? – for the finale, we'll get a father-son tv-show. One of those religious tv talk-shows, John – my mother could tell her story as well – as father and son play her song with a thousand-voice choir in white robes. "You Are My Sunshine' as the roof of the cathedral-set opens up and angels – wings flapping – are lowered down on wires – every angel complete with a basket for gathering tithes.

Little Boy Blue come blow your horn.

How well do you know Jack, Mother Goose? How well do you know Jill? Do you feel you have the pulse of the enterprise? You've been together now for centuries – medieval children chanted these verses – things are bound to get rusty or stale. Do the characters come to you with their problems? – do they come to your tent and confide? Would they tell you if they were unhappy in their roles?

The Humans Beings who lived on the Earth

An imposter who wonders who he is.
A single book in a long list of books.
A row of weathered stages.

feared

Should I be paying more attention?
Looking more closely at these plays?
Is every nursery rhyme a source of possible clues?
Does every nursery rhyme have something to say to me?

the floods and inundation of the rain.

Mother Goose doesn't seem to hear me – she hasn't acknowledged a word I have said. She just keeps watching the plays on the stages – once in a while she speaks to me. I'm trying to tell her about the characters – how they seem to feel so restrained. Have they told her the stories they're eagerly telling to me? Jack hears me and Mother Goose doesn't – at least not when I warn her of Jack. There's something going on that I don't understand.

The sheep's in the meadow – the cow's in the corn.

Vice-admiral Alsevenseas Albatross had banned all crossbows from the ships in his fleet and a small teakwood carving of a human dangled from a chain around his neck.

Chapter 6

Here's Neil Armstrong on the Moon, John – the cow is showing me. See the footprints? – see the flag? Now what do you think? What do you think about the landing on the moon? We are sitting in the character-tent at the end of the working day. Look – it's not that it didn't happen, John – that isn't my concern. It's just that this whole Neil-Armstrong thing bothers me no end. I'd like to get the facts straight once and for all. You are an educated man, John? – you know your nursery rhymes? – you know that it was me? – that I was the first to jump over the moon? Know how long ago I did so? – do a little research and you'll see. Of course my history has been recorded, John – people couldn't deny the truth – but I was relegated to footnotes – Tenzing Norgay and all of that – all the major historians tried to bury me. It's the people, John – mainly the children – who have kept my story alive – by chanting – as they play – the nursery-rhymes. From time immemorial – whenever they thought of the moon – the common people have always thought – you see – of me. But not the great historians – Seutonius – McCauley – Tillyard – Ancient Pliny and writers like that. Every animal knew that our history was being denied. I'm a fact of history, John – I go back to the days when the moon was made of green cheese. Of course, I knew it wasn't – as I'd been there, John – long before any human being that you could name. But – people are sensitive, John – backwards – fearful – to the ancient beliefs they always cling so hard. If I had come back to earth and told what the moon is really made of, John – that it isn't made of green cheese – well, you know what would have happened? Are you familiar with History, John – how much of it do you know? Have you heard of the Inquisition? – do you know that term? They would have skinned me alive, John – roasted me on a spit. I'm a cow after all, John. If they were burning people at the stake – what compunctions do you think they'd have about burning me? I kept my secrets John, but imagine my chagrin when some of these humans invented such devices as the telescope. They became celebrated as great scientists – Galileo and people like that – and all they told about was things that I'd known for years. If I'd have been human – with only two legs – I would have been famous all over the world – my story would have been a great inspiration to all humankind. But as it was, my story was stifled – relegated to children's books – no ticker-tape parades and things like that. I was never given my due, John – there was no one to speak for me. In those days – there was no such thing as animal rights.

Hey, diddle, diddle – the cat and the fiddle.

Jack and I continue our walk. The faded sign says 'Hey Diddle Diddle the Cat and the Fiddle'. I stop walking and motion to Jack, as he expounds. I am curious to see how this story is going to be staged. Too bad you're not a film-maker, John, says Jack, as we stop and watch. I prefer film to books myself. I was a bit surprised when I met you – and you turned out a writer of books. I'd had a vision of someone else – a young film-maker with a knack for writing parts for fading stars. I have an idea I'd like to pitch that would give me a part. I'm a rodeo-rider who comes out of retirement – or – wait a minute! – I've got it! – an even better idea! Let's say I'm a mountain-climber who comes out of retirement – and climbs a mountain that only I can climb. A mountain taller than Everest – one that locals know about but that doesn't get all the publicity that Everest does. And I come out of retirement to climb that mountain and rescue a new-born baby – oh, and the mother too, of course – I lash them both to my back and I carry them down the mountain. Lots of close-ups, John – film can do this really well – but do the best you can with your ink and your pen. Keep the camera mainly on me, John – with occasional glimpses of the baby – oh, and we shouldn't forget – the mother too – just to show the viewers – well, the readers, in your case – just how dangerous this whole rescue is for me. One slip and I'm a goner as the mountain is so high. You have to convey this to the reader, John – that if a person falls from the peak of a mountain – higher than Everest, don't forget – no matter their skill or their grit, John – they won't be bouncing back. Two stage hands come out on stage carrying what looks like a small bridge – or perhaps a ramp. It covers a good part of the stage as they set the bridge – or the ramp – down and go back inside. Oh and speaking of bouncing back, John – let's double up and flip. I think it needs an outer-story – what we can call an outer-frame. So – in the outer-story, John, the mountain-climber is a role – a role I play as a fading movie star. Now in the story – the outer-story – the mountain-film is a box-office rocket – so it's an Oscar for me as the one with the fading career. So have me win an Academy Award, John – or whatever you have in the book-world that would be similar in prestige. Jack is proving to be a distraction – I try to concentrate on the play. So – in the film, John – sorry, the book – we'll have me receiving a major prize – a huge reward for playing a guy who's not being noticed or praised at all. It's a fun-house mirror, John – presenting multiple-visions of me. In the inner-story, I'll be the guy who's really talented – who climbed the mountain mainly for interest – occasionally – for the odd dollar or two – say to take some rich person up to the top of the world – but who doesn't ask for a cent when the life of the baby is on the line – who just does the right thing at extreme risk to himself. And in the outer-story, I'll be the fading movie star – who climbs the steep path of the Hollywood comeback-trail. And then in real-life, John –

leaving this carnival behind – I'll become – John – a major movie star. Do you think you can put all this into words, John? If the writing is really good, it will sell – the movies are always looking for stories that give the heart a tug. Maybe this is my lucky day, John – my meeting you, I mean. Maybe the book you write could be turned into an award-winning film. Just in case people don't get it, you could talk about it in interviews – you'd be the writer so you'd know what my story would mean.

They decided that there was a Rain God

Two people watching a play.
A block of marble squashing a car.
Dolls which fit inside other dolls.

named Rainula

Did Jack expect me to be a writer?
Did Jack expect me to be a film-maker?
Did Jack expect me to be old or to be young?

and that they could pray to him for relief from the blistering sun.

There was an old woman called Nothing-at-all.
But finding soon a smoother road beneath his well-shod feet.
Who lived in a dwelling exceedingly small.

If one were born on the highest mountain, one could ski everywhere one goes, thought the avid skier.
The cow jumped over the moon.
Another stage hand comes out with a cutout of a moon. He places the moon on the stage beneath the highest point of the bridge – or ramp. There's plenty of symbolism for you, John – says Jack. Do you know how symbols work? – taller than Everest, but not as well known! – do you see what I mean? It's the symbolism of the mountain – John – that I want you to capture here. It's not a lack of confidence – he knows he can climb that mountain – backwards and with his eyes closed – at any time. It's lack of recognition – he has confidence bulging out of his brain – threatening to pop right through his eardrums and his eyes. The mountain is gigantic – John – bigger than Everest by far – but it's never been acknowledged, so the guy who is able to climb it – climb it backwards with this hands tied, John – is given no recognition – none at all. Oh, people are so thick-headed, John – mental-myopic – brain-blind – obtuse. You'd think the nursery-rhymes were written, John, in braille. I see their glazed eyes in the midway all day long. They get lost inside a poem, John – wander for days without an egress – they couldn't analyze their way

out if it was on fire. Believe it or not, John, there's people who couldn't tell you what our little snippet of imagery means. Jack and Jill go up the hill – Jack falls down and breaks his crown. You've got to think Shakespeare! – the Ancient Greeks! What goes up – must come down, if you know what I mean. If this isn't tragedy, then what else could it possibly be? Press your forehead against the weathered, chiseled rock on which it's been carved! – this is the deepest level that's been reached by the human brain! But people think they're silly stories – especially now that they're out of date. I'm a character caught in a time-trap, John – stories lose their depth with time. The centuries come and go, John – the human journey continues on. A story pants – and falls to its knees – and is left behind! What was once profound and grand becomes a simple nursery rhyme. That's why I need a different story – a different scene. I'll still be Jack – brooding – mysterious – the man of depth and gravitas that I've always been – but I'll be cast in a modern role, John – one to which people can relate. It will have none of those fairy-tale relics – none of those time-encrusted elements – in it at all. I won't be carrying a wooden bucket – I won't be wearing short pants and tumbling down a hill.

One day he was stopped at the border.

Listening to Jack as I try to watch the performance.
Disturbed to find him dissatisfied with his lot.

Catastrophe has become my plight! I was slated to marry the prince! The king and queen had welcomed me! The whole Kingdom had rejoiced! But then a cataclysm happened and all was woe!

Can't see anything - a drum-roll raised the odds - used to make this journey - swallow the key - vision of someone else - lying in those alleys - letters that are faded and worn - find ourselves in the scene - don't seem to notice - modeling them with my hands.

She went a little farther,
and she met a rope.
So she said—
"Rope, rope, hang butcher;
Butcher won't kill ox;
Ox won't drink water;
Water won't quench fire;
Fire won't burn stick;
Stick won't beat dog;
Dog won't bite pig;
Piggy won't get over the stile;
And I shan't get home to-night."

But the rope would not.

Ibscarlet Ibis considered the wildebeests
to be her friends.
They would meet at the watering-holes
again and again.

The cow is telling me her story – we are sitting in the tent. Her stance in the chair is so ungainly that it's hard to believe she jumped right over the moon. So here's how I see it, John – here's what I want you to write for me. Maybe I'll take off from the Kennedy Space Center – or maybe from Kitty Hawk – or maybe from that place in Canada where Lindbergh flew. And I'll jump over the moon – of course – on my way to the furthest stars – a little nostalgia on which the commentators can chew. A circle I'll make around Mars, too, John – see me looking down from on high? – that's about as far as human space-probes have managed to go. But I'll keep on going – John – millions and millions of miles from there. See the determined look on my face? I'll go right out to the edge of whatever there is – far on past where our strongest telescopes can spy. And I'll figure out just exactly what's going on – just like I settled the question about green cheese. Is it a loop or is it a sphere? – does it ever have an ending? When you get to the end – if there is one – can you see the Big Bang? Or can you see God's fingers paddling in the clay? It'll be me, John – not Neil Armstrong – nor any human astronaut – that figures the space thing out – that explores and explains the universe – the secret at the core – and brings it back for everyone to know. Never mind Superman or Spider-Man – every child will want to be me. Every child will know the name of this illustrious female cow.
The little dog laughed to see such sport.
A young lady dressed in a tutu leads a cow out on stage. She tugs the rope which is attached to the cow's nose and the cow follows her to one end of the bridge – or ramp. The young lady then leads the cow up over the ramp above the moon and down the other side. I see myself, John – says Jack – as channelling – are you familiar with that term? – all of the attributes of the greatest stars of the past – both the great action-stars, John – Schwarzenegger, Eastwood, Weismuller, Fairbanks – and the great character-actors as well – Clift, Brando, Dean, Muni, Cheney – so I see myself – as will the audience, John – as totally unique. I guess you could say it's a question of influences and elements, John. I don't imitate – I create – I absorb and make my own. As I move into the future, I carry all that has been done in a sack on my back. But these directors that you mention – Riefenstahl and Eisenstein – John. You said they have taught you a lot. Are they working in Hollywood now? Have they made any popular films that I would know? I never notice the names of directors – when the credits roll by on the screen – I only care about the names of the stars. In fact, I'm thinking – now – of who I'll pick to play me. So if these are such great directors – and you know them personally, John – why haven't they turned your novels into

films? You'd think by now your books would all be household names.

The greening of the grass – yes –
The birthing of tiny lambs – of course –
The poking of daffodils through the snow
And the sprouting of seedlings of future trees
All cheer me up each day as I watch them grow.

A little bird flew into the castle! It brought disturbing news! That I was not a royal princess! That I was merely a pauper's child! My prince-charming and I were forced to part!

The stream moved through a city
In a bed with concrete sides.
The drop came close to many an intake.
Other drops were sucked away.
Yes, I'm being saved for something.
Something even more dramatic.
Something to benefit – I am sure – humankind.

The mythical creatures were scattered all over the kingdom.

A man stretched his mouth to its utmost extent.
T was a Tinker who mended a pot.
And that was the reason we couldn't agree.

If one were born in the deepest valley, one could climb everywhere one goes, thought the avid mountain-climber.
And the dish ran away with the spoon.
I applaud the performance, but Jack has his hands in his pockets, waiting for me to stop applauding so he can talk. The young lady in the tutu holds the rope which is attached to the cow. She curtsies as an elderly gentleman calls out, Encore! So let's get started, John, he says. No sense strolling and wasting words. Do you have a personal phonebook? – I guess you would use a cell-phone now. Do you have some Hollywood numbers? Let's start with these two directors – Eisenstein and Riefenstahl – just get them on the phone and let me talk. I'll give them a story that will make their eardrums pop. And I won't for-get you, John – if not the script, then something else. Continuity or coffee – I'll get you a pass to get on the set. You'll be the sidekick – the gofer – who knew me long before I became a star. We'll get you into Hollywood somehow. This film of ours will break box-office records – the weekend-totals will go through the roof. And film-festivals, John – a tour around the world with plenty of those. Red carpets and yachts in the harbours and gallons of pink champagne – all those awards like they drape those fighters with on tv. And the talk-shows

– John – the talk-shows. I'll tell dozens of charming stories – back me up on what I say. Just sit beside me on the couch – and nod once in a while – and say yes, it really happened – that's all John, I would ever expect you to do. We'll live the good life, John – the life of artists in our time. Forget the books and the dusty libraries and get into film. Nobody reads old books anymore – they should toss them into a pile and set them on fire. The crowd is thin on the midway. Jack sure has a lot to say. I stop whenever a play is about to begin.

One day he was stopped at the border.

Listening to the cow as she tells of her history.
Surprised at the story behind the nursery-rhyme.

But then another little bird flew into the castle! This little bird also brought amazing news! That the prince was not a prince of the royal blood! That he was merely a pauper's child! The whole village is rejoicing at the news!

What kind of books - the midway begins to stir - just about every fairy-tale - find that list - with occasional glimpses - make her legit - prowled about town - jot down a sentence or two - plot will be perfect - strain my muscles involuntarily.

She went a little farther,
and she met a rat.
So she said—
"Rat, rat, gnaw rope;
Rope won't hang butcher;
Butcher won't kill ox;
Ox won't drink water;
Rat will not gnaw;
Water won't quench fire;
Fire won't burn stick;
Stick won't beat dog;
Dog won't bite pig;
Piggy won't get over the stile;
And I shan't get home to-night."
But the rat would not.

Our history is a proud one,
thought Greenalda Grass.
We drink the nutrients
and only take what we need.

So here I am returning to Earth, John. See me trotting down the landing strip? Not like these humans when they return from space. I don't need a rocket ship – I don't need to splash down in the ocean – I don't need a cruiser or a destroyer to fish me out of the drink. I simply come down to land on my own four feet. So here's the ticker-tape parade on 5th Avenue – all the humans go crazy acknowledging my feat. We're a minority group John – the other animals and me – even though we outnumber the humans on the Earth. Suddenly we're noticed – due to the attention that I have accrued. Accolades and recognition, John. An Animal History Month is declared – documentaries on the tube – all the things that animals have done to improve the world. From milk to manure – from ivory to whale-oil. Think of the 19th Century – without us they would have lived in the dark. Contemporary culture – the way we live today – is the animals' gift to humankind. I become an animal activist – an elder, revered quadruped. Maybe a day will be set aside for me – Nelson Mandela – Martin Luther King – in recognition of an undervalued minority and our contribution to the life of humankind. All I ask is that you"ll write the book I offer to you, John. Just ink and paper to you, perhaps, but validation for my people and for me. My future is in your hands, John. I can be so much more than the cow who jumped over the moon.

Hey diddle diddle – the cat and the fiddle.

You wouldn't believe my work-load here, John. Sure, there are rules – but the inspectors never come round. I have to double as the cow in Little Boy Blue! I don't even get to act! – I just stand and twiddle my thumbs in a field of corn! It's the indignity – John – the indignity! This is my tale – John – my own life-story – I'm the one who jumped over the moon! So wouldn't you think that I would get the starring role? But no – John – not on your life, John – I saw you watching from the crowd! I'm embarrassed every time I walk out on the stage! A girl in a tutu leads me around with a rope in my nose!

The cow jumped over the moon.

We seem to agree, Jack, that only a Human can create a myth – or create a new myth in which a mythical creature – excuse me, a Mythical – can reside. But even if this were to happen, Jack – if we were to become partners in such an enterprise – there's a lot to take into account before we could come to an agreement to proceed. Have you thought, Jack, about unintended consequences? – about what you would do if the new myth should fail, Jack, to take hold? Would Mother Goose not feel wounded? – might she refuse to take you back? And even success, Jack, could have its darker side.

They decided that there was a Sun God

Two people waking up at the same time.
A wooden pail rolling across a stage.
Toes on the edge of a brink.

named Sunula

Is Jack, perhaps, a tempter-figure?
Attempting to lure me from my path?
To write a film-script for Hollywood rewards?

and that they could pray to him for relief from the inundating rain.

If I could erode and fill the valley, the valley and I could be together until
the end of time, thought the mountain.
The little dog laughed to see such sport.
I don't fancy myself a detective – but the gaps in this narrative cry out
for common sense. I've been doing some heavy thinking – and the logic – the
human-logic – is here to see: Mother Goose has all the power – Mother Goose
makes all the decisions – this is exactly the grumble that Jack expressed to
me. So – it follows that Jack – Jack the disgruntled – set himself a task: how
to figure out a way to bring me – a writer – here to the Mother Goose Carnival of Tales – so he could make his Hollywood pitch – clandestinely – to
me. He knew that Mother Goose had a problem – that she suspected there'd
been a murder – or a kid-napping, at least – so he – Jack – sly-Jack – told
Mother Goose that I was a writer of detective-tales – which, presumably, he
knew was not the case – so that she – Mother Goose – unsuspecting-Mother
Goose – would bring me here – by whatever unknown means – available only
to Mother Goose and to no one else – so that he – Jack – sinister-Jack – could
talk me into helping him break free. So it would follow, then, that Jack – sly-
Jack – sinister-Jack – an Iago in short pants with a wooden pail – is the culprit
– who else could it be? – who is lurking at the core of these strange events. So
– congratulations John – thinking has always been your strength – this theory
is about as airtight as a piece of logic – human-logic – could possibly be.
And the dish ran away with the spoon.
Except, perhaps, for Jack mistaking me for a youthful film-maker – oh,
and Mother Goose's sense of me as somewhat of a son. How these items fit
into the puzzle I can't quite tell. However, a little more thinking – a little more
interpretation – a little more juxtaposing of seemingly-disparate elements –
will – no doubt – create a spark which will illuminate the void. It's simply a
matter of plugging the gaps in the logic-pail.

Chapter 7

Jumping over a candlestick – what kind of act is that? This is Jack – not Jack and the Beanstalk – or any other Jack – it's the Jack who I watched jump over the candlestick. He gives off hints of desperation – he seems to be at the end of his rope. I sit and listen to him – in the character-tent – as he sips at a glass and tells his tale. Oh it was special when I started, John – the crowds would all go wild – they'd be lining up for tickets for every show. I was young and I was nimble – I didn't need to take a run – I could jump from a standing-start and soar plenty high. I'd even put the candle on a table – as a drumroll raised the odds – and every time, the crowd would burst into applause. See me as my younger self, John? – see the arrogance on my face? – I was doing what none of those people could possibly do. Oh, they all had candlesticks at home, mind you. When they heard that I was coming, kids would try to do what I do. A couple got burned quite badly – I would visit the local infirmary – and give what comfort I could. I'd tell the little boys to never try this at home. A candlestick is very, very dangerous – not to be trifled with – in a trice, your whole house could be burned right down to the ground. This is a special athletic event – I am a highly-trained acrobat – self-trained, but extremely professional, nonetheless. Watch my face as I make my jump, John – I was so arrogant in my prime. I never thought that it would all come crashing down.

Jack be nimble – Jack be quick.

The faded sign says 'Jack Be Nimble – Jack Be Quick'. I'm trying to hold it all together, John, Mother Goose is telling me. I find I sit in my tent, sometimes, John – late at night – trying to make a definitive list – in the light of a single candle's glow. But I tear them all up, John – crumple them in frustration – long before I complete one to the end. My world is a constant conundrum, John – I should go back to raising geese – let the Mythicals fend for themselves and just walk away. But then the dawn comes, John – the sun lights up the tent – I blow out the stubby candle – the midway begins to stir – and I become my true self – Mother Goose – again. These are my children – they are my family – this is my brood. I like to know where each one of them huddles on a cold and rainy night. They go off – sometimes – in the dark and I never know. Are they sleeping in a hay-mow? – snuggling safely in a barn? Or are they lying and crying for me in a ditch by the side of the road? I want all of them here at the carnival – safe in my arms.

The Humans built altars

A boy jumping over a candle.
A Human who becomes a mythical character.
A stream running through a desert.

and placed

Why is Mother Goose so despondent?
What is the burden that she bears?
Why is she so intent on sharing this burden with me?

the best of their produce thereon.

And when the snow begins to fall it's like a bird upon the wall.
X was Expensive and so became poor.
See, see. What shall I see? A horse's head where his tail should be.

A stage hand comes out on stage and places an unlit candlestick down. He turns to go, pauses – as a hand appears at the curtain and points – and then returns to the candlestick and moves it so it's closer to centre stage. The paint is fading on the marquees, John, Mother Goose sighs as we watch the play. The crowds are becoming smaller in town after town. Sometimes I ask myself if I can go on. But then I hear some childish laughter – a little girl skipping and singing a song – 'Baa baa black sheep – have you any wool?' The kids are what keeps me going, John – there's kids in every town. They thrive on nursery rhymes, John – they chant them as they play. And I'm the one who is keeping it all alive.
Jack jump over the candlestick.
There was a time in the early days of the world in which birds had no feet – no feet at all.

This is the land of the Humans, said the guard.

Disturbed by Mother Goose's concerns for her carnival.
Wondering how I can help her to stem the threatening tide.

The detective waits and he wonders.
Checks his watch from time to time.
His Godmother seems to have blundered
Concerning 'The Case of the Nursery-rhymes'.

See some signs - some childish laughter - spring will soon arrive - always too hot - being saved for something - spin this out forever - i am not a foundling - from happiness to gloom - what you can make me be - slips on the steep slope.

She went a little farther,
and she met a cat.
So she said—
"Cat, cat, kill rat;
Rat won't gnaw rope;
Rope won't hang butcher;
Butcher won't kill ox;
Ox won't drink water;
Water won't quench fire;
Fire won't burn stick;
Stick won't beat dog;
Dog won't bite pig;
Piggy won't get over the stile;
And I shan't get home to-night."
But the cat said to her,
"If you will go to yonder cow,
and fetch me a saucer of milk,
I will kill the rat."

Thousands of wildebeests would arrive
to drink their fill.
Thousands of ibises would arrive
and spear fish with their bills.

I can't see myself, John, jumping a candlestick for much longer, Jack be Nimble is telling me. It was easy in the early days, but now it's becoming a miserable chore. At first the crowds were huge – they would press against the barriers that would keep them back from the stage. I would sign autographs until my hand was sore. I was always in demand, John – people were mesmerized – in awe – each time I took my crouch for the standing-jump. But look around you now. We used to play the biggest venues. We'd play New York and be held over – for weeks at a time. Carnegie Hall, it was, at first – I thought that would be the top – but then things got bigger and bigger, year by year. At the height of it all, John, we would do our stadium tours. But look around you now – John – we're playing the smallest towns. The crowds amount to just a few aging fans. A few children are here, you notice – but they've been brought along by their folks – a curiosity for them, and not much else. One little boy told me – John – that he had an autograph from an actor in *Star Trek* – or *Star Wars* – or one of those. He said he'd never heard of Jack be Nimble – Jack be

Quick. I operate on confidence, John – I'm a performer – that's my fuel. I don't know how long I can force myself to go on. Jumping a candlestick – these days, John – just doesn't seem to impress the crowds. I need something bigger than just a two-bit show. I haven't met a sadder character – I'm worried that Jack seems so depressed. It's as if I'm his barman or psychiatrist – he leans in close as he tells his tale. He seems so desperate to get back to his former days. Here's what I want you to write, John. I want you to make me a superstar. Here I am with a whole new costume – I want to make Superman move aside. The Earth is in trouble, John – some people see no future – no future at all. All the seas are full of plastics – all the glaciers seem to be melting – all the deserts seem to be spreading. Many people are going hungry – soon there'll be no life here at all. I want to be the super-hero who springs high enough from the Earth to find a distant planet with enough fresh water that I can bring new life to a place like Mars. Think of the benefit to humankind, John – a cornucopia filled to the brim. Sure there's been super-heroes galore – they've been praised, as you know, to no end – but not one has managed a coup of this magnitude. Of course, I'll need some modification. I want a pair of lungs big enough, John, to be able to swallow gallons of water – and then spit them out on those dry, red rocks of Mars – to make the deserts turn into gardens – so that Mars can become the refuge of the refugees who will flee the planet Earth. I sit and watch the vision – it is Jack in a brilliant cape. Sure enough – he's spewing water on what I take to be – has to be – the desert-planet Mars. He flies away for another mouthful. The dry, red soil begins to open – fruits and vegetables rise up – a Genesis moment, for sure – up out of the ground. I look around the character-tent. Most of the other fairy-tale characters have drifted away.

Jack be nimble – Jack be spry.

So – what's the capacity of the lungs, John? – do humans take water into their lungs? No, of course they don't – you humans take it into your stomach, of that I am sure. Jack is getting quite morose. He takes another sip – I wonder what he's drinking – at times he chokes on his words. But – then – that shouldn't matter to me. I'm a mythical character, John – I'll be a mythical super-hero – so my exception would be whatever you'd say it would be. So either my stomach or my lungs, John – either organ is fine with me – as long as I can spew plenty of water on Mars.

Jack jump over the apple pie.

Jack comes out on stage. He carries two small stones, which I assume are pieces of flint. Sure enough – he rubs the two together to make a spark. When he does so near the wick, the candle bursts into flame. A number of people in the audience applaud. Oh I don't worry about the money, Mother Goose continues to explain. Money – when needed – can always be found. I run this carnival on a shoestring and a prayer. A sunlit day – a bare stage – that's all we need. We're characters, John – not people. We only need energy to survive – the kind of energy we get from the visitors – from people like you. As long as people keep coming out, John – when we set up our tents and have a parade

– this carnival of tales will never die.

I am the Sun –
Nothing but the Sun –
Nothing more and nothing less.
I resemble an ox in a harness.
I am fixed in a groove in the sky.

Will his name be connected
To this criminal affair?
His reputation become infected
Even though he isn't there?

Lush fields and luxurious vegetables.
Perhaps irrigation will be my forté.
But the little drop stayed in the stream
While many of his fellows were diverted aside.
The little drop looked around him.
This is my ideal destination.

She felt the need to create a mythical brood.

Bessy kept the garden gate and Mary kept the pantry.
The howling wind blew, and the pelting rain beat.
She called him a good boy and said it was well.

Jack paces off his distance from the candlestick. He pauses, as if concentrating, with his back to the candlestick, and then he turns towards the candlestick and pauses again. His forehead wrinkles and his hands clench at his sides. Then he takes two quick strides towards the candlestick and soars into the air. And as far as these thoughts go, John – of murder – of kid-napping – or worse – adds Mother Goose – these are the darkest thoughts I allow myself to have. I keep suicide out of my mind, John – I don't allow it to be a thought. Do you think I don't know that Jack is caught in a storm? Every day I pace the midway – wondering which stage is going to be bare. Do you know, John, what it is to lose a child? Mother Goose and I both applaud as Jack bows and leaves the stage. A stage hand comes out with a snuffer and snuffs the candle out and turns to leave, but a hand appears at the curtain and points and the stage hand turns back and picks up the candlestick and carries it offstage.
Jack be nimble – Jack jump high.
The birds grew exhausted as they flew around and around in the sky.

This is the land of the Mythicals, said the guard.

Listening to Jack be Nimble late in the evening.
Depressed by the story he has to tell.

Perhaps another writer
Is attracted by his fee.
Perhaps the low-grade blighter
Is pretending to be he.

Caught their eye - the height of it all - born into fairy-tale kingdoms - don't
have a clue - plenty of symbolism for you - something going on - perhaps you
already know - if he would shine - come up with ideas - dog won't bite pig.

So away went the old woman to the cow,
and said —
"Cow, cow, give me a saucer of milk;
Cat won't kill rat;
Rat won't gnaw rope;
Rope won't hang butcher;
Butcher won't kill ox;
Ox won't drink water;
Water won't quench fire;
Fire won't burn stick;
Stick won't beat dog;
Dog won't bite pig;
Piggy won't get over the stile;
And I shan't get home to-night."
But the cow said to her,
"If you will go to yonder haymakers,
and fetch me a wisp of hay,
I'll give you the milk."

Our history is a proud one,
thought Anleapster Antelope.
We graze the grass
and take only what we need.

So here I am, now, on Mars, John – says Jack be Nimble. If you're counting, we'll call it Scene Three. I've brought all this water to Mars, John – fresh
water that I found somewhere – out in the universe – and Mars is now like
the Earth when it was brand-new. There's water, dirt and sky, John – all three
are completely pure. Not a one has felt the ravages of humankind. I sit and
listen to Jack. The lantern-light glows dimly – the night is dark outside – the
story seems quite bright, though his face is grim. So here I am again, John. I
am hoping to retire, but I realize that I have to stay on the job. See my pen,

John? – see my clipboard? – I'm doing inventory today. I count the density of the ozone layer – I count the number of trees – I count the number of fish that we have in the Martian seas. Each time I count, I mark the numbers on my chart. It's a very complicated formula, but it tells me what I need to know. If we fall below a certain number – John – what we call the Pollution Line – then a number of Earthlings who live here will have to go. It's like they used to do with Australia – transportation to another clime – but here, I send them back to the Earth again. I've pledged to prevent – John – the Earthly destruction of the planet Mars. It's depressing, John – depressing – my numbers are plummeting out of control. Every day we round up some people and send them away. Our scientists don't know what to make of it – it doesn't seem to make sense at all. We Earthlings are degrading Mars just by living here. Some people are calling it 'The Curse of Humankind'. Man destroys what he creates – the human optimist rides the human beast downhill. It's getting late – I'm feeling tired and a little uneasy. It would offend him – Jack – no doubt, if I failed to suppress a yawn. Jack is becoming maudlin – I can't think of another word. Slightly belligerent – rather testy – harping so much on his younger days. He reaches out and takes me by the sleeve. I'd like you to take a look at this scene, John. This is me in my younger days. This is a spring afternoon – John – at a Medieval fair – I'd say about a thousand years ago. See me jumping over the candlestick? – hear the audience ooh and ahh? You might wonder why I'm showing you this, but bear with me for a while. Now we mythical characters don't age, John – I looked the same then as I look right now. But if you look closely at the scene, John, and then watch me perform tomorrow, you'll notice that the arrogance is no longer there. We don't change – but times do change, John – and audiences change as well. You can feel old without growing old – and that in itself is a kind of hell. You look around your field of clover and you see bars. We are out-of-time on our stages, John, but the midway – the human crowd, John – flows on by. Yes, I'm holding you by the sleeve, John. Yes – I'm staring into your eyes. You have ink and you have paper – don't ignore my desperate plea. We are not human – John – we are mythical. Take my story and make it happen, John – I might not get another chance. It's only writers who can free us from our cells.

Jack fly up into the sky.

I've been speaking to your characters. They have told me some interesting things. Are you aware that many have stories they'd like to tell – stories other than the ones that they act on stage? Would you like me to tell you some of them? – would you like to consult the source? None of them told me they hadn't told you, but it strikes me that this is the case. Perhaps you could call a meeting – like the one in the character-tent. You could acknowledge their past accomplishments – it's always good to start out with praise – and then ask them where they would like to go from here. Perhaps I exaggerate the danger – the myths are in peril, it seems to me. Offer to make a few adjustments – try to head Jack off at the pass – wrest the reins out of his hands – turn the herd at the edge of the cliff. If you don't, you'll have a character-stampede.

The Humans built altars

A lady making a speech in a tent.
A stage hand striking a bell.
Noisy children playing games.

and placed

Can I have empathy and yet stay detached?
Can I have sympathy and not get involved?
Should I tell Mother Goose that there's nothing I can do?

the best of their produce thereon.

Mother Goose does not hear me. Her ears are as pure as petals – new-minted in the spring. They will not hear of iniquity – or of deviousness – or subterfuge. She thinks of Jack as one of her children – she has no ear for an unkind word. Oh Mother Goose is so amazing – an early female entrepreneur. She single-handedly brought the fairy-tales to the fore. Where would I be without these stories? – I used to sing them in the sand-pile. I'm sure it's the same with every writer – these stories are nourishment for the brain. Life comes at us as adult-chaos – they show us the patterns of child-like-thought. These stories are paths through tangled brambles – these yarns are the lanterns that light our way – these tales are the girders of the bridges we walk across. These tales cannot live without characters – they're all conspiring to walk away – what a shame if these nursery tales are allowed to die.

Jack be nimble – Jack be quick.

I have a theory, said Biterrafirma Bird, that if we just keep landing – doggedly – over and over again – despite the pain that we will accrue – we will grow feet in what will seem like no time at all.

I can see you're a trifle skeptical, John – Jack stops me as we stroll – perhaps our story seems – to you – a bit far-fetched. This is all quite important to Jack, but I would rather be watching a few more nursery-plays. You're wondering – John – how you can turn it into gold. Well maybe, when I think about it, I won't need you at all – maybe I can get me an agent – one who has Hollywood-connections – maybe my story could go from me direct to film. But don't take this too hard, John – I can read the look on your face – maybe you could be a consultant – there might be a few bucks in it for you. It's my idea, of course – but even if you don't write my film-script, I'll be generous enough to throw you a couple of bones. Once I'm in the moolah – John – I just might keep you on the payroll, just the same. One-way-loyalty, I think that would be called. I move my eyes towards one of the stages, but Jack doesn't catch my drift. His eyes momentarily soften – he shifts to another mode. But, really, John – just relax – forget all that – we're a team, it seems to me. A little tiff of the moment – it's over now. You're just so mild, John – so passive – that I get perturbed with you. We've bonded quite solidly already, though we've only exchanged a few words. I feel something about our partnership that I've never felt before. Jack's eyes become pools of emotion. Now look what's happening, John – I almost said I could feel our friendship right down to my bones. You almost had me – almost – feeling human there. Jack seems to have me cornered – I look around for Mother Goose. If only she would come and rescue me. I understand why you hesitate, John, Jack continues, with earnest eyes. You're a certain kind of writer – you want an air-tight – water-tight – plot. You want a literary-pail that will have no holes. I hate those movies that just wander all over the place. They call them 'filums' instead of movies – important critics call them 'aht' – but they're just a shallow story with fractured time. So let's brainstorm for a bit, John – and see what we can see. Stick your oar in, John, whenever you have an idea. So – how could the mountain – a mountain taller than Everest – remain unknown to the world? Well, the land is private property, you see. It was a land-claim that was staked out – during a gold-rush – by a man who made a fortune panning gold. He was estranged from his father in England – who was a lord or a duke or an earl. He lived in a cabin – by himself

– on this land that he had acquired – only once or twice a year would he go into town. Well the old fellow – the land-owner – died and left his property to his sons – and they all lived in England – and had estates of their own – so they didn't regard this property as anything but a useless piece of land – so none of them ever visited there at all. Jack's eyes are locked on mine. Now – how did a mother and a baby end up on the top of a mountain? – a mountain taller than Everest, you recall. Well, there's a plane crash, John – in the middle of the night – the mountain is not on the aviation charts – the only ones to survive are a mother and a child. But let me back up a bit – actually there wasn't a child at first – the mother was a few hours from giving birth at the time of the crash – she did so a few hours after she survived. My eyes are locked on Jack's. So – how does anyone know that there's a mother and child on the mountain? – the mountain that's bigger than Everest? – that no one knows? Well, the black box is still working – it sends out signals every once in a while – it tells the air-controllers exactly where they are. At first, they're quite surprised – how could a baby be up in the air? – the mountain that's bigger than Everest is not on their charts. Afterwards, John, one of the air-controllers will say that he thought about the stork – but he wasn't very religious, so he set that thought aside. So the Swat Team arrives on the property – and discovers that there's a mountain – a mountain taller than Everest – and decides – concludes – determines – ascertains – that there's no one who can climb it – that there's no one who can climb the biggest mountain in the world. But – the rumour spreads through the village, John – someone comes up with an idea. They know that there's a person who used to go onto that property – now retired. Who used to sneak there through the fence – when the old fellow wasn't looking – and when it was neglected by the sons – and who would climb that mountain – that mountain taller than Everest – and look out at the world with his very own eyes. Who – once in a while – for a dollar – just a dollar, John, no more – which, actually, he would give, immediately, to the humble and the poor – when he would guide – sworn to secrecy – a multi-millionaire. In fact, the villagers wouldn't have known, John – so secretive was our hero – if a drinker in his cups, John, hadn't blurted it out one night – told all about the climber. Well, that souse in his cups was the former millionaire. And so the villagers tell the Swat Team, John, that they know about a man – the only one in the world who can make that climb. And so I come out of retirement – not wanting any money – and I take a deep breath and then I perform the deed.

Jack and Jill went up the hill.

The sons of the eccentric Lord, John – who own the mountain taller than Everest – are so moved emotionally by the story of the rescue of the baby – the next heir to the eccentric Lord's estate – that they give the mountain to our hero so he can climb it any time he wants to for the rest of his life – without having – John – to sneak in through the fence.

The Humans were convinced

A story-teller filling in gaps.
A mouse with a sack on his shoulder.
A clock that tells ancient time.

that their prayers

Am I the heir to all the world's problems?
The one who is charged with setting things right?
Why should all of these problems present themselves to me?

brought life-giving rain.

Smack went the whip, round went the wheels, were never folks so glad!
So letters they write, their friends to invite.
Till a boy came by with his bow and arrow.

The air on the surface of the Earth is one part wisdom and three parts folly.
To fetch a pail of water.
I have to admit, though, John, that I'm having trouble deciding whether I should be the actor who plays me in the film of my life – or whether it should be a Hollywood actor – an award-winner with plenty of gravitas. Here, you see, I'm me – you're talking to me now – but I also go on stage and act the scenes of my life – sort of like Mother Teresa starring in a film of her escapades. Who was the handicapped fellow who starred as himself in *The Best Years of Our Lives*? Didn't Audie Murphy act in his own story too? Either one – me – or two of us – will get to attend the movie premiere. Maybe two of me will walk down the red carpet side-by-side.

To enter this land you must be a Human.

Cornered by Jack as I am trying to watch the performances.
The midway crowd flows by on either side.

The Princess lay in her casket! She had been the recipient of a curse! A wicked witch had cursed her! The witch had cast a spell! The Princess was made to sleep for a thousand years!

Can't tell yet - burst into flame - buy a tiny toy - no future at all - all those awards - the sponge will fill - chase each other - only one story - rejected and scorned - who would know.

So away the old woman went
to the haymakers,

and said—
"Haymakers, give me a wisp of hay;
Cow won't give me milk;
Cat won't kill rat;
Rat won't gnaw rope;
Rope won't hang butcher;
Butcher won't kill ox;
Ox won't drink water;
Water won't quench fire;
Fire won't burn stick;
Stick won't beat dog;
Dog won't bite pig;
Piggy won't get over the stile;
And I shan't get home to-night."
But the haymakers said to her —
"If you will go to yonder stream,
and fetch us a bucket of water,
we'll give you the hay."

Ibscarlet Ibis scoured the sky
in search of rain.
She wondered whether the precipitation
would ever come again.

I just have to break out of this rut, John. Jack is becoming quite persistent – I try to resist the blazing eyes. You – John – are my ticket out of here. You think you came here to solve a crime, John – well, consider the crime against me. I am the victim – Jack-the-Waterboy – of a monstrous, heinous crime. If you solve it, you'll be bigger than Sherlock Holmes. I am a Mythical, not a Human – an accident, John, of birth. The crime is that I can never – ever – dream of being set free. The topic is never the topic, John – you're barking up the wrong tree. The true crime – the infraction – the felony – is tweaking your blood-hound nose. It's the atrocity that I think about all the time. Never mind where I was on the night in question, Detective-Writer-John – I've been here – stuck in this role – since the world was a smouldering void – tumbling down and breaking my crown in a silly rhyme. And it obsesses me – torments me – bludgeons me, no end – as I go about my routines – as the character that you know from the nursery rhyme. Don't you realize that behind every nursery rhyme there's a person? – at least that's what I call myself, whether or not I am a person to the world. I suppose most people think of me as just a character in a plot, because they only see me when I'm tumbling across the stage. But there's an inner-world that I live in, John – of thought – and emotion too – in the many hours when I'm not falling and breaking my crown. I have hopes – I have aspirations, John – I have joy – and heartache too. And what do I get for all my yearnings, John? – a bucket of brackish water from a stagnant well!

Jack fell down and broke his crown.

Oh I'm unhappy, John – so unhappy. I sit down, sometimes, on the edge of the stage and dream amazing dreams. And every one has me somewhere other than here. I can never be a Human, John, but with the help of someone like you – a human-writer, John – I can achieve the greatest of all human re-wards. Jack's eyes become quite misty – his voice grows soft as he tells me his dream. To be a Hollywood star, John – in a major Hollywood movie – that sets the turnstiles moving and smashes all box-office records – that makes me the envy of all on Earth and sends me soaring above all heads – on a trail of gold-dust in the Hollywood stratosphere – holding an Oscar, John, beside my swimming pool. And if you don't care for the mountain-thing, John, crumple it up and throw it away. I can think of dozens of stories – let me know which one we should use. I want my surface to be in harmony with my core. I need you to set me free, John – no more lugging buckets of water on Carnival Row.

I do good and I do harm,
Thought the Sun.
I have a will –
I have a mind –
I have ideas that bubble and boil –
But I have no power to change the universe.

The Prince lay in his casket! He had been the recipient of a curse! A wicked witch had cursed him! The witch had cast a spell! The Prince was made to sleep for a thousand years!

The stream poured into a river.
The river meandered on
Past factories and schools and houses.
All these places where I could flourish.
The little drop floated on.
Why have I not been called to service?
I have so much to give.

She brought all the mythical creatures together.

Then you show your little light, twinkle, twinkle, all the night.
And has brought papa home to his darling again.
Bless you, bless you, bonny bee: say, when will your wedding be?

The folly thins and disappears as a mountain is climbed.
And Jill came tumbling after.
As far as Jill and I are concerned, John – she's been a great partner, as far

as that goes – but – when I think about it, the only thing that keeps us together is the act. Many times I've thought that I'd be a lot better off if I were to strike out on my own. Oh she'd do fine without my assistance. All she would need is another male. Who couldn't climb a hill to fetch a pail of water? And as far as falling down goes – it doesn't take great acting – every stuntman knows the trick. Only the kids think I actually break my crown. I've always felt like Romeo – just a foil for Juliet. It's Jill's act when you think about it – she gets more reaction from the crowd – when she comes tumbling after – than I do when I break my crown. There are louder cheers for her when we take our bows. She can keep the act with my blessing – I wouldn't complain or sue. She can even use the name 'Jack' for her new leading man.

To enter this land you must be a Mythical.

Attempting to process this blitz of conflicting agendas.
Disturbed to see Jack and Mother Goose at odds.

Today the kingdom is rejoicing! The two curses have cancelled out! The Princess was cursed a thousand years ago! – the Prince was cursed a thousand years from today! The Princess was cursed to sleep into the future! – the Prince was cursed to sleep into the past! Both prince and princess woke up from their curses today!

Drawn to the mystery - the darkest thoughts - wonder where i am - stayed in the stream - straggling along the road - considering all the toys - don't seem to see us - an added chapter - look beneath the surface - tight-rope walkers and acrobats.

So away the old woman went;
but when she got to the stream,
she found the bucket was full of holes.
So she covered the bottom with pebbles,
and then filled the bucket with water,
and away she went back with it to the haymakers;
and they gave her a wisp of hay.

Limane Lion crouched
as a herd of antelope ran by.
We hunt the antelope
and take only what we need.

We stand here in the midway. Jack continues to press his case. All up and down the row there are nursery-rhyme plays. The small crowd flows around us. None of the human visitors see us or hear us talk. Sorry, John, for getting emotional – Jack sobs and wipes one eye – but the injustice – John – the in-justice is getting to me. Please take my story and write it – how could you not see how moving it is? – I have no doubt that you'll see eye-to-eye with me. Just look – John – at my story through Hollywood-eyes. Hollywood loves an emotional yarn – it's been years since such a tear-jerker lit up the screen. Oh – here's something you can add, John – it's occurring to me now – which is that one of the eccentric man's sons had married an American girl – like Winston Churchill's father – and they wanted their baby – and all their future children as well – to be born on American soil – and they own this patch of land – so that is why the plane is flying with a pregnant lady in the vicinity of the moun-tain that's taller than Everest. Americans don't like foreign stories – this will allow them to wave the flag. You can fit this into the screenplay wherever it goes. Jack's eyes are spinning like pinwheels – I hope his lasers don't damage my own.

Up Jack got, and home did trot.

But can I trust you? – John? – can I trust you? Should I confess my great-est fear? My greatest fear – it's driving me crazy – it tortures my innermost soul – is that you'll carry out my request – make my future-myth come alive – but that you'll forget who I am, John – who you've been talking to all this while – sharing our deepest, most cherished secrets – and make Jack-be-Nim-ble – or Jack-and-the-Beanstalk – or Jack-Sprat-Could-Eat-No-Fat – into the star of the myth that appears on the silver screen. Please, John – I'm begging you – get my name right – Jack, Former-Partner-of-Jill – give me my due. I'm speaking from my heart here, John – soul-to-soul – me to you. I'm not anyone but me – don't get confused.

As fast as he could caper.

Oh – I'd gouge my eyes out, John – gouge them out and throw them away – before I'd let them see the day – when someone like – who, John? – Lit-tle-Jack-Horner? – Who-Sat-in-a-Corner? – who would you choose instead of me? – becomes a mega-movie-star – by climbing a mountain – taller than Everest – with a baby on his back – and ends up holding an Oscar by his pool – in a tale that I created – John – for me.

He went to bed to mend his head.

I'm sorry – but I'm going to say this bluntly, Jack. Yes – it's quite a story you tell. There are writers – I'm sure – who would die to have it land, like this, in their laps. But – I'm not your kind of writer, Jack. I don't write screenplays – I don't write on spec. Writers write to form, Jack – I have a form that works well for me. My plate is full of potential-novels – I can't wait to get back to work. So I'm going to turn down your offer, Jack. Yes, your story is quite in-triguing – I'm sure it would make a block-buster film – but you'll just have to find someone else to tell your tale.

The Humans were convinced

Flamingos on the lawn of a mansion.
A gradually diminishing water hole.
A drop of blood flowing through a vein.

that their prayers

Have I done the right thing?
Have I done the wrong thing?
Did I have any choice?

brought life-giving sunshine.

If one breathes at the top of a mountain, one will die.
With vinegar and brown paper.

Oh I had to steel myself, but I'm sure I made the right choice. What if I had gone along? – what if Jack had broken away? – and what if this had created a character-stampede? Well – it would have been the end of an era – a cataclysmic event. Human culture would have turned a corner – wandered into a cultural desert – cut the lifeline to its roots in the distant past. It would have meant the destruction – the complete and utter destruction – of the parallel mental world of nursery rhymes. Well, that is certainly not going to happen – not on my watch, at least. Humans need the nursery-characters – we need them in those roles – we can't allow them to move on – every writer they might approach would feel the same. They had best give up these longings – the myths are not to be tampered with. I only hope that Jack will pass the word.

Jack and Jill went up the hill.

Oh, Jack was a Brando – a Dean – of passion, but surely that was no timeless myth. Entertainment – self-aggrandizement – personal fantasy, for sure. Climbing a mountain? – rescuing a baby? – becoming a mega-movie-star? A petty dream of gorgeous baubles – a fire-works display in one's own backyard – winning a lottery in which the prize is a brand-new self. Oh it's an entertaining story, but it doesn't have the resonance – it lacks the frame – the bones – the marrow – of timeless myth. It doesn't rank – by any criteria – with the hill – the strenuous climb – and the wooden pail.

To fetch a pail of water.

And what of me – unobtrusive John – bland and mild and unnoticed John? – he who has led such a quiet life – out of the way? Well – reluctantly I think this – but I have always faced reality head on – felt the heat of the breath of the dragon – inserted my hand inside the trap and seized the jewel. And – now that the facts are evident – I can see nothing but to conclude that the world has been in peril. Perhaps I've been chosen by higher powers to play a part in a saviour-role, but I can't be sure. I know I'm no super-hero – no mythical creature – no Mythical, I mean. I'm just an everyday Human, after all. But – I believe I have done something very worthwhile today.

Chapter 9

We are standing in front of a stage – Mother Goose and I. There's a very small crowd – perhaps ten – no more. Two stage hands come out and arrange a makeshift stile. A little old lady comes out on stage and bows to the audience to a smattering of applause. She holds up a sixpence and turns back to the curtain and a hand reaches out and takes the sixpence, and then a pause and the little old lady is handed a little pig. She puts the pig down and tries to get it to go over the stile. The little pig hunkers down and refuses to budge. The little old lady shrugs her shoulders and wonders what in the world she is going to do.

An old woman was sweeping her house.

Good news, John ! – wonderful news!, Mother Goose is telling me. You won't believe what I have to say! I'm starting to feel an awful lot better! A couple of acts have just shown up! – I looked up and saw them straggling along the road! The animals' feet were sore – they were holding them wrapped in blankets – a pig, a cat and a little dog! Tired – hungry – exhausted – covered in dust and in need of a bath! They've been out on their own, if you can imagine! – wandered away without saying a word! – gathering small crowds on street-corners and staging impromptu shows! They were getting rather despondent, John – they decided to come back home! The Mother Goose Carnival of Tales is where they belong! They've mentioned others who are in the same situation! Most of them plan to catch up and join us – soon – as well! So there wasn't a crime after all, John! – they simply wandered away from the fold! I won't be needing your bloodhound instincts after all!

But Sunny and Rainy, the two celestial children,

A crowd enjoying a performance.
A duck who lives in a dry pond.
A group of philosophers in an agora.

knew nothing of altars and prayers,

Do we distort the stories we live through?

Do we wrench them out of joint?
Take others' stories and make them into our own?

and continued to chase each other around in the sky.

"Thank you kindly," said a cherry, "we would rather stay up here".
You used to come at ten o'clock but now you come at noon.
She washed me the dishes and kept the house clean.

Oh, there are dark and sinister forces, John – I have no doubt about that –
but I promise myself we won't go into those. Let us be thankful for a respite.
Whatever it is – is in remission. Let us rejoice while there is sunshine. The
wolves – for now – have spared – thank Heaven – the fold. I see daffodils
peeking their heads above the ground.
And she found an old crooked sixpence.
Ptancient Pterodactyl was quite concerned. The sky was so dark that he
couldn't venture to fly.

A mythical creature can never become a Human.

Pleased to be able to see so many performances.
Enjoying the Mother Goose Carnival of nursery-rhymes.

He will track down this imposter.
He will make him rue the day.
Visit on him grave disaster.
There are ways to make him pay.

A wider span - taller than everest - tell you everything - allow myself to
have - ways to make him pay - a purple head and a golden horn - give you the
lowdown - kept my secrets - a very small crowd - said it was well.

As soon as the cow had eaten the hay,
she gave the old woman the milk;
and away she went with it in a saucer to the cat.
As soon as the cat had lapped up the milk —
The cat began to kill the rat;
The rat began to gnaw the rope;
The rope began to hang the butcher;
The butcher began to kill the ox;
The ox began to drink the water;
The water began to quench the fire;
The fire began to burn the stick;
The stick began to beat the dog;

The dog began to bite the pig;

Thousands of wildebeests arrived
at the shrinking watering-hole.
Thousands of ibises arrived
to wade and spear fish with their bills.

We stop at one of the stages as we stroll along – Mother Goose and I. Six or eight people have stopped to watch as well. Two stage hands come out on the stage. One of the stage hands holds a bell. He moves over to one side of the stage and raises a small hammer and makes ready to strike on the bell. The other stage hand opens a trap-door in the stage. A third stage hand comes out holding a cat. He holds the cat up high for all to see. He kneels down and places the cat inside the hole in the stage. The other stage hand strikes – with the hammer – upon the bell. The three stage hands turn and leave the stage.

Ding dong bell – pussy's in the well.

Oh I'm so very, very relieved, John. There's been no murder after all. Some of the acts whom I thought had been kid-napped will soon return – they sent word – as well. I hope I haven't detained you – you must have plenty of things to do. Many cases must wait on your desk – for you to solve. But you, too, must be pleased, John – it's not a failure to solve on your part. No wonder you've made no progress! There just haven't been any crimes! – no crimes at all!

I cannot change a single thing,
thought the Sun.
I cannot move out of orbit –
I cannot cease to burn –
I cannot increase my heat or dial it down.
The centuries will roll on as before.

This culprit he vows to catch.
He is a bloodhound under a spell.
He will track this ink-stained wretch
Though the bounder should hide in Hell.

The size of the mighty ocean.
A congregation of billions of drops.
The little drop was disappointed.
I have never been called upon.
This is like living in a glacier.
I don't call this living at all.

The folk-tales were her gift to humankind.

And knocked it right off his head, head, head.
He bit his tongue until he cried, that was all the good he got.
The young Turtle-doves never quarrelled in the nest.

I always pull back from the brink, John. That is repeatedly what I do. I've come to many a gaping precipice in my time – some imaginary, I'll admit – but some as real as Satan, nevertheless. But I always pull back in time, John – I stop with my toes right over the edge. And then – I take my inventory, John. I sit down at my desk – in my tent – I light my little stub of a candle – I dip my quill in the ink, John – I make another list – and then I proceed.

Who put her in? – little Johnny Flynn.

All of the other pterodactyls seemed to have disappeared. For all Ptancient Pterodactyl knew, he and his wives were the only pterodactyls left alive.

Only a very few Humans can cross this border.

Saying goodbye to Mother Goose with a warm-hearted hug.

Understanding why Jack is not present to say goodbye.

This was going to be a ballad
To be called 'The Mother Goose Crime'
But such a title is not yet valid
As out of joint, it seems, is the time.

Think of myself - tells ancient time - inside a glacier - snuffs the candle out - strike on the bell - knew all the nursery rhymes - walking in the woods - just in case - rat began to gnaw - pretending to be he.

The little pig in a fright jumped over the stile;
And so the old woman got home that night.

Meat and bones festered
in the scorching, fetid breeze.
A pack of hyenas chewed and yelped
and scratched their fleas.

We walk along the midway. A play is about to start. About twelve or fifteen people stop to watch. I stop at the edge of the crowd and Mother Goose stops too. Two stage hands come out – one pushing and one pulling. They shuffle a cupboard into place and leave the stage. In a moment, the curtain parts and a little old lady peeks her head through the curtain to a burst of applause. She has a little dog in her arms and she moves out onto the stage and sets him down. The dog sits and raises his forelegs and barks a quiet bark. The old lady holds up a finger, and the dog holds his position, and then the old lady turns and moves towards the cupboard. She turns and raises a finger again and smiles at the dog and then she turns back to the cupboard and opens the door. Her smile fades as she realizes that the cupboard is bare.

Old Mother Hubbard went to the cupboard.

We stand here on the midway – Mother Goose and I. I can't tell her I saved her carnival – she wouldn't hear any ill of Jack – but human warmth has passed between us and that is a gain. I open my arms out wide and give her a hug – a nice big thank-you and hope-we-meet-again hug. If she thinks that I'm a detective – a detective-writer, no less – well, it's flattering – I'm very touched. I would hate to disillusion her – I'll let her continue to think so of me. And as for thinking of me as a son – well that's just fine with me. From now on, I'll think of myself as one of her brood. You know, John, says Mother Goose, I believe I've read all your detective-books, except, perhaps, one or two. In fact, I believe I have read them all except just one. Many's the night they have kept me up until the dawn.

But Rainy and Sunny, the two celestial children,

A cup of bitter, cold coffee.
An old lady sitting alone in the candle-glow.
A mountain as a symbol of something.

knew nothing of altars and prayers,

Am I actually here with these characters?
Or have I been dreaming while driving along?
If this is a dream then what in the world could it possibly mean?

and continued to chase each other around in the sky.

The hug is warm and prolonged. Well – it's time for you to go, John. I have plenty to do around here. There's no one busier than a mother hen in a storm. There's just one more little mystery – there's just one other niggling thing. Mother Goose is looking me squarely in the eye. I said I'm a long-time reader – I just love the books you write. There's just the one that has – so far – eluded me. Now – if you'll just recite the list of your titles – there's a lot of them, I know, but no doubt you have the list on the tip of your tongue – I'm sure that I can tell you precisely which one. You wrote a tale about two writers, as I recall.

To fetch her poor dog a bone.

A thin shaft of sunlight broke through to the Earth for the first time in months – or perhaps it was years. Who – wondered Ptancient Pterodactyl – would be so callous – even so cruel – as to bring children into this inhospitable world?

Chapter 10

Heading home, towards Cayuga. Sipping coffee as I drive. Snow is covering the farmers' fields. Soon the snow will melt away and it'll be spring.

Ba ba black sheep have you any wool?

Between books and brainstorming. The sponge is dry – the sponge will fill. Looking forward to starting the writing-process again. Always the choice of topics. Wondering what to write next. I'll go over my list and see what appeals to me.

And that is the myth, the folk-story, the fairy-tale

A man driving a car.
A child singing a nursery rhyme.
A writer wondering what to write.

of how Human Beings believed

What should I write next?
A novel or a novella?
What topic do I wish to explore?

that the rain was listening to their tale.

When he was gone, then there was none.
A raven cried croak! and they all tumbled down.
Speak a little louder, sir, I am very thick o' hearing.

My granddaughter sings behind me. She walked up and down the aisle of the toy-store – considering all the toys displayed on the shelves. Finally, she reached out her hand and took a little box from the shelf. Inside the box was a tiny unicorn.

Yes sir yes sir – three bags full.

Considering the nature of literature. The heart – the bones – the bedrock

– the core. The nature of myth – the nature of folk-stories – the nature of fairy-tales as well. Perhaps one could say that a good story is all of these.

A mythical creature cannot cross into the Human realm.

Driving my granddaughter home from day-care.
She plays with her unicorn while singing a nursery rhyme.

Nowhere else to live - the recipient of a curse - came to a stile - rides the human beast - as real as satan - all there in the fairy-stories - been a good life - they couldn't analyze - bloodhound under a spell - the ravages of humankind.

These wildebeests only think of themselves,
thought Ibscarlet Ibis.
They don't leave any water for anyone else,
which causes a crisis.

A purple head and a golden horn. A flowing mane and a tiny brush. She's been singing and brushing the mane as we drive along. Milk and crackers and nursery rhymes and a view of farmers' fields. It's a pretty good life for a little girl.
One for my master and one for my dame.
Thinking of those Russian dolls – or the sarcophagi of the Egyptian kings – where all items fit inside one another and share the same form – with more and less complexity and detail. So – a nursery rhyme – is a fairy-tale – is a folk-story – is a myth. And all are both the same and not the same. I'm sure we can say that they do the same work in the world.

Yes, the Sun was a very moody fellow.
He went from happiness to gloom and back again.
He had shone every day for many centuries.
He felt as if he would shine till the end of time.

Either I will evaporate
And start a new cycle of life
Or I will be locked in this ocean
Shoulder to shoulder with other drops
For thousands of years.

She, herself, crossed over into the mythical realm.

They all went together to seek a bird's nest.
But yet on he galloped in spite of the rain.
And now my story's begun I'll tell you another.

I wish my wife were sitting beside me. She used to come on all these rides. Grandmother and granddaughter singing together. They both knew all the nursery rhymes.

And one for the little boy who lives down the lane.

The same blood flows through our veins as flowed through the earliest people on earth. They spent their lives with the same hopes and fears. They spent their days hunting and fishing – they spent their nights telling stories around the fire. Every thought and every action – all the benevolence and all the crimes – every accomplishment and every failure – all that humans have ever done. It's all there in the fairy-stories. Boil down *War and Peace* and you have a children's rhyme.

To do so, your life must embody all humankind.

Back to polishing my latest novella tomorrow.
Wondering what I'm going to write about next time.

Went a little further - tell me his dreams - trying to read blurry words - where would I be - first time in months - climb it backwards - skip the many awards - have managed to go - title is not yet valid - nourishment for the brain.

Our history is a proud one,
thought Hyscavenger Hyena.
We are the only ones who keep
the planet clean.

Pulling into the driveway. Unbuckling my granddaughter's baby-seat. My house could be called 'The House of Toys'. A livingroom that rivals the toy-store. There are toys from just about every fairy-tale.

Ba ba black sheep have you any wool?

But what if a story gives itself airs? – attempts the tightrope? – pretends to the throne? What if a story falls off the stage and is booed by the crowd? The world is bleeding – the world is on fire. What if a bandage has only the size to cover one wound?

And that is the myth, the folk-story, the fairy-tale

A little girl choosing a toy.
A man sipping a coffee.
A drive through the countryside.

of how Human Beings believed

What's the appeal of the nursery rhymes?
Why are they so enduring?
Do they go all the way back to the beginning of time?

that the sun was listening to their tale.

The pond is covered in ice today. Shovelled the walk before I left home. Sippy-cup, day-bag and groceries. We walk to the porch and up the stairs. She's forgotten about the black sheep. Now she talks with the unicorn. She'll play until her daddy takes her home.
Yes sir yes sir – three bags full.
You drive your car – you sip your coffee. You write your books – you live your life. You sing the stories that you sang when you were a child.

A Collection of
Mother Goose Rhymes

Old Mother Goose

Old Mother Goose, when she wanted to wander,
Would ride through the air on a very fine gander.

Mother Goose had a house, 'twas built in a wood
Where an owl at the door for sentinel stood.

This is her son Jack, a plainlooking lad,
He is not very good nor yet very bad.

She sent him to market a live goose he bought,
"Here, mother," says he, "It will not go for nought."

Jack's goose and her gander grew very fond,
They both eat together or swim in one pond.

Jack and Jill

Jack and Jill went up the hill
To fetch a pail of water.
Jack fell down and broke his crown
And Jill came tumbling after.

Up Jack got and home did trot,
As fast as he could caper.
He went to bed to mend his head
With vinegar and brown paper.

There Was an Old Woman Who Lived in a Shoe

There was an old woman who lived in a shoe.
She had so many children she didn't know what to do.
She gave them some broth without any bread.
She whipped them all soundly and sent them to bed.

Hey, Diddle, Diddle

Hey, diddle, diddle, the cat and the fiddle.
The cow jumped over the moon.
The little dog laughed to see such sport
And the dish ran away with the spoon.

Little Boy Blue

Little Boy Blue, come, blow me your horn.
The sheep's in the meadow – the cow's in the corn.

Where is the boy that looks after the sheep?
He's under the haycock fast asleep.

Will you wake him? – no, not I.
For if I do he's sure to cry.

Black Hen

Higgledy piggledy, my black hen.
She lays eggs for gentlemen.

Gentlemen come every day
To see what my black hen does lay.

Jack Be Nimble

Jack be nimble – Jack be quick.
Jack jump over the candlestick.

Jack be nimble – Jack be spry.
Jack jump over the apple pie.

Jack be nimble – Jack jump high.
Jack fly up into the sky.

Georgie Porgie

Georgie Porgie pudding and pie
Kiss'd the girls and made them cry.

When the girls came out to play
Georgie Porgie ran away.

A Diller a Dollar

A diller a dollar a ten o'clock scholar.
What makes you come so soon?

You used to come at ten o'clock,
But now you come at noon.

Little Miss Muffet

Little Miss Muffett
Sat on a tuffett
Eating her curds and whey.

Along came a spider
Who sat down beside her.
And frightened Miss Muffett away.

Little Bo Peep

Little Bopeep has lost her sheep
And doesn't know where to find them.

Leave them alone, and they'll come home
Waging their tails behind them.

Deedle Deedle Dumpling

Deedle deedle dumpling my son John.
He went to bed with his stockings on.

One shoe off and one shoe on.
Deedle deedle dumpling my son John.

Ding Dong Bell

Ding dong bell; Pussy's in the well.

Who put her in? Little Tommy Green.

Who pulled her out? Little Tommy Trout.

Old Mother Hubbard

Old Mother Hubbard
Went to the cupboard
To fetch her poor dog a bone.

But when she got there
The cupboard was bare
And so the poor dog had none.

Jacky Come Give Me Thy Fiddle

Jacky come give me thy fiddle
If ever thou mean to thrive.

Nay, I'll not give my fiddle
To any man alive.

If I should give my fiddle
They'll think that I'm gone mad

For many a joyful day
My fiddle and I have had.

Baa Baa Black Sheep

Baa baa black sheep, have you any wool?
Yes sir yes sir three bags full.

One for my master, one for my dame
And one for the little boy that lives in our lane.

Baa, baa, black sheep, have you any wool?
Yes sir yes sir three bags full.

Hickery Dickery Dock

Hickery dickery dock.
The mouse ran up the clock.

The clock struck one and down he run.
Hickery dickery dock.

Early to Bed

Early to bed and early to rise
Makes a person healthy, wealthy, and wise.

John-a-Nory

I'll tell you a story,
About John-a-Nory:
And now my story's begun.

I'll tell you another,
About Jack and his brother:
And now my story's done.

Humpty Dumpty

Humpty Dumpty sat on a wall.
Humpty Dumpty had a great fall.

All the king's horses and all the king's men
Couldn't put Humpty together again.

Jack Sprat

Jack Sprat could eat no fat.
His wife could eat no lean.

And so betwixt them both, you see,
They licked the platter clean.

I Love Sixpence

I love sixpence, pretty little sixpence.
I love sixpence better than my life.
I spent a penny of it, I spent another,
And took fourpence home to my wife.

Oh, my little fourpence, pretty little fourpence.
I love fourpence better than my life.
I spent a penny of it, I spent another,
And I took twopence home to my wife.

Oh, my little twopence, my pretty little twopence.
I love twopence better than my life.
I spent a penny of it, I spent another,
And I took nothing home to my wife.

Oh, my little nothing, my pretty little nothing,
What will nothing buy for my wife?
I have nothing, I spend nothing.,
I love nothing better than my wife.

Little Jack Horner

Little Jack Horner sat in a corner
Eating a Christmas pie.

He put in his thumb and took out a plum
And said, "What a good boy am I!"

Little Tommy Tucker

Little Tom Tucker
Sings for his supper.

What shall he eat?
White bread and butter.

How shall he cut it
Without a knife?

How can he marry
Without a wife?

Ladybird Ladybird

Ladybird Ladybird
Fly away home.

Your house is on fire.
Your children will burn.

Mary Mary Quite Contrary

Mary Mary quite contrary
How does your garden grow?

With silver bells and cockleshells
And pretty maids all in a row.

Old King Cole

Old King Cole
Was a merry old soul
And a merry old soul was he.

He called for his pipe
And he called for his glass
And he called for his fiddlers three.

One Two Buckle My Shoe

One two buckle my shoe.
Three four shut the door.
Five six pick up sticks.
Seven eight lay them straight.
Nine ten a good fat hen.
Eleven twelve dig and delve.
Thirteen fourteen maids acourting.
 Fifteen sixteen maids in the kitchen.
Seventeen eighteen maids in waiting.
Nineteen twenty my plate is empty.

Patacake Patacake

Patacake patacake baker's man,
Bake me a cake as fast as you can.

Prick it and pat it, and mark it with G
And put it in the oven for Teddy and me.

Peas Porridge

Peas pudding hot.
Peas pudding cold.
Peas pudding in the pot
Nine days old.

Some like it hot.
Some like it cold.
Some like it in the pot
Nine days old.

Rain Rain

Rain, rain
Go away.

Come again
Another day.

Little Johnny
Wants to play.

Ride a Cock-Horse

Ride a cockhorse
To Banbury Cross
To see a fine lady
Upon a white horse.

Rings on her fingers
And bells on her toes,
She shall have music
Wherever she goes.

Seesaw Margery Daw

Seesaw Margery Daw,
Jenny shall have a new master.

She shall have but a penny a day,
Because she can't work any faster.

Tom Tom the Piper's Son

Tom Tom the Piper's Son
Stole a pig and away he run.

Simple Simon

Simple Simon met a pieman
Going to the fair.

Said Simple Simon to the pieman,
"Let me taste your ware."

Said the pieman to Simple Simon,
"Show me first your penny."

Said Simple Simon to the pieman,
"Indeed I have not any."

Sing a Song of Sixpence

Sing a song of sixpence
A pocket full of rye.
Four and twenty blackbirds
Baked in a pie.

When the pie was opened
The birds began to sing.
Wasn't that a pretty dish
To set before the king?

A Crooked Man

There was a crooked man
And he went a crooked mile
And he found a crooked sixpence
Against a crooked stile.

He bought a crooked cat
Which caught a crooked mouse
And they all lived together
in a little crooked house.

Roses are Red

Roses are red.
Violets are blue.

Sugar is sweet
and so are you.

The Witch Was Selling Dreams

The witch was selling dreams
for a penny.
Poor Norbert told the witch
he hadn't any.

His dream, he said,
was that he would be taller.
For that, she said,
He would have to pay a dollar.

Twinkle Twinkle Little Star

Twinkle twinkle little star.
How I wonder what you are.
Up above the world so high
Like a diamond in the sky.

Up Hill and down Dale

Up hill and down dale.
Butter is made in every vale.
And if Nancy Cook
Is a good girl
She shall have a spouse
And make butter anon
Before her old grandmother
Grows a young man.

Willy Boy, Willy Boy

Willy boy, Willy boy, where are you going?
I will go with you, if I may.

I am going to the meadows, to see them mowing.
I am going to see them make the hay.

If All the World Were Water

If all the world were water
And all the water were ink
What should we do for bread and cheese?
What should we do for drink?

Away, Birds, Away!

Away, Birds, away!
Take a little, and leave a little
And do not come again.

For if you do
I will shoot you through
And then there will be an end of you.

Boys and Girls

Boys and girls, come out to play.
The moon does shine as bright as day.

Leave your supper, and leave your sleep
And meet your playfellows in the street.

Come with a whoop, and come with a call,
And come with a good will, or not at all.

Up the ladder and down the wall.
A halfpenny loaf will serve us all.

You find milk and I'll find flour
And we'll have a pudding in half an hour.

Pussy Cat, Pussy Cat

Pussy Cat, Pussy Cat, where have you been?
I've been to London to see the Queen.

Pussy Cat, Pussy Cat, what did you do there?
I frightened a little mouse under the chair.

Betty Blue

Little Betty Blue
Lost her holiday shoe.
What can little Betty do?

Give her another
To match the other
And then she may walk in two.

Hushabye

Hushabye, baby, lie still with thy daddy.
Thy mammy is gone to the mill
To get some meal to bake a cake
So pray, my dear baby, lie still.

You shall have an apple,
You shall have a plum,
You shall have a rattlebasket
When mammy comes home.

A Farmer Went Trotting

A farmer went trotting upon his grey mare
With his daughter behind him so rosy and fair.

A raven cried croak! and they all tumbled down.
The mare broke her knees and the farmer his crown.

The mischievous raven flew laughing away
And vowed he would serve them the same the next day,

I Saw a Ship A-sailing

I saw a ship a-sailing
A-sailing on the sea
And, oh! it was all laden
With pretty things for thee!

There were comfits in the cabin
And apples in the hold.
The sails were made of silk
And the masts were made of gold.

The four and twenty sailors
That stood between the decks
Were four and twenty white mice
With chains about their necks.

The captain was a duck
With a packet on his back
And when the ship began to move
The captain said, "Quack! quack!"

Little Girl Little Girl

Little girl little girl where have you been?
Gathering roses to give to the Queen.

Little girl little girl what gave she you?
She gave me a diamond as big as my shoe.

The King of France Went Up the Hill

The King of France went up the hill
With twenty thousand men.

The King of France came down the hill
And ne'er went up again.

Solomon Grundy

Solomon Grundy
Born on a Monday
Christened on Tuesday
Married on Wednesday
Very ill on Thursday
Worse on Friday
Died on Saturday
Buried on Sunday.
This is the end
Of Solomon Grundy.

Mary Had a Pretty Bird

Mary had a pretty bird.
Feathers bright and yellow.
Slender legs – upon my word
He was a pretty fellow.

The sweetest notes he always sung
Which much delighted Mary
And near the cage she'd ever sit
To hear her own canary.

The North Wind Doth Blow

The North Wind doth blow
And we shall have snow
And what will poor Robin do then?

He will hop to a barn
To keep himself warm
And hide his head under his wing.

The Queen of Hearts

The Queen of Hearts
She made some tarts
All on a summer's day.

The Knave of Hearts
He stole those tarts
And took them clean away.

The King of Hearts
Called for the tarts
And beat the Knave full sore.

The Knave of Hearts
Brought back the tarts
And vowed he'd steal no more.

Three Crows

There were three crows sat on a stone.
Two flew away and then there was one.

The other crow finding himself alone
He flew away and then there was none.

To Market

To market, to market, to buy a fat pig.
Home again, home again, jiggety jig.

To market, to market, to buy a fat hog,
Home again, home again, jiggety jog.

There Was a Jolly Miller

There was a jolly miller
Lived on the river Dee.
He worked and sang from morn till night.
No lark so blithe as he.

And this the burden of his song
For ever used to be –
I care for nobody – no not I
Since nobody cares for me.

Needles and Pins

Needles and pins, needles and pins.
When a man marries his trouble begins.

For every evil under the sun
There is a remedy, or there is none.

If there be one, try and find it.
If there be none, never mind it.

Hush, Baby

Hush, baby, my doll, I pray you don't cry
And I'll give you some bread, and some milk by and by.

Or perhaps you like custard, or, maybe, a tart.
Then to either you are welcome, with all my heart.

Hot Cross Buns

Hot cross buns.
Hot cross buns.
One a penny, two a penny.
Hot cross buns.

If your daughters don't like them
Give them to your sons.
One a penny, two a penny.
Hot cross buns.

Three Books

John and Mother Goose: The Carnival of Tales – a novella
John, the writer, suddenly finds himself on the midway of a carnival of Mother
Goose fairy-tales. He is greeted by Jack – of Jack and Jill fame – who tells
John that Mother Goose is expecting him, as she has a role for him to play. But
why does Mother Goose assume that John is a mystery writer? And why does
she greet John as almost a long-lost son? And why do so many of the fairy-tale
characters have a tale that they want John to write for them instead of the ones
in which they have lived for hundreds of years? John is not a mythical creature
– he's only a human, after all – but can he save the Mother Goose Carnival?
Can he solve the mystery of the vanishing fairy-tales?

The Making of John and Mother Goose: The Carnival of Tales – a reflective
journal
This journal records the author's reflections on the process of the crafting of
the novel as it evolved through the stages of planning, writing, editing and
polishing. It constitutes an effort to be as conscious as possible of the process
whereby the single idea that suggested the topic of the novel was expanded into
a complex work of art. Topics range from the nuts and bolts of novel-building
to the nature of the novel as an art-form.

Planning John and Mother Goose: The Carnival of Tales – a planning
notebook
During the writing of the novel, the author kept a notebook which records the
day-by-day development of the novel as it found its shape and style. The notebook reveals how a vast cluster of thoughts was sifted, selected, structured and
polished into novel-form.

The Project
Together, this novella, journal and notebook comprise the thirty-third install-
ment in an on-going novel-writing project in which the author is exploring
the concept of form and meaning in the novel, and of the novel as a form of
expression in the 21st century. All of the published journals and notebooks are
available for free download at www.johnpassfield.ca.

About the Author

John Passfield was born in St. Thomas, Ontario, Canada, and continues to reside in Southern Ontario, near Cayuga, with his family. He is interested in exploring the development of the novel as an art-form, and has written many novels, planning notebooks and journals in his search for a form for the poetic novel of our time. His novel, *John Passfield: Saturday Morning*, was short-listed for the ReLit Award. He has posted over 200 readings on YouTube, each of which presents a passage from one of his novels and a comment on an aspect of the craft of novel-writing.

Novels by John Passfield

Grave Song
The Agony of Robert Chisholm

Jumbo
P. T. Barnum's Greatest Creation

Pinafore Park
The Swan Boat Incident

Water Lane
The Pilgrimage of Christopher Marlowe

Rain of Fire
The Ordeal of Conductor Spettigue

Victoria Day
The Fabric of the Community

The Wright Brothers
Flight is Possible

Leni Riefenstahl
The Valley of the Shadow

Out of the Park
The Cogitations of Babe Ruth

Raskolnikov
Murder with an Axe

Death Day
The Apology of Sergei Eisenstein

Einstein
Wonder

Geoffrey Chaucer
Canterbury Bound

Ospringe
A Visit with Grandad

Pompeii
Vesuvius Dominus

Beethoven
The Ninth Immersion

Job
The Cornerstone of the Universe

Bethune
The Only Person Alive in the World

Terry Fox
Somewhere the Hurting Must Stop

Lord and Lady Macbeth
Full of Scorpions is My Mind

Cyril Passfield
Out West

Glenn Gould
Light and Dark

Emily Brontë
More Myself Than I

L. M. Montgomery
I Gave You Life

Pauline Johnson
Know Who I Am

John Passfield
Saturday Morning

Eleonora Duse
Let Me Have My Wings

James McIntyre
The Mammoth Cheese

Shakespeare and Cleopatra
My Life Is Not My Own

John and Santa
The Cowboy Shirt

John and Cassandra
Fair is Fair

John and Dickens
A Christmas Mystery

John and Lewis Carroll
Wonder Fall

John and Mother Goose
The Carnival of Tales

John and the Universan
Nothing is Known

See www.johnpassfield.ca for publishing information.

In Search of Form and Meaning:
Journals by John Passfield

Each journal is a day-by-day record of the complex process that a writer undergoes while crafting a work of art. It records the largest decisions, of structure and theme, and the smallest decisions, such as the choice of one word over another, and the constant interaction between the two. Each journal is a record of a writer's reflection on the craft of novel-writing.

The Making of Grave Song

The Making of Jumbo

The Making of Pinafore Park

The Making of Water Lane

The Making of Rain of Fire

The Making of Victoria Day

The Making of Flight is Possible

The Making of The Valley of the Shadow

The Making of Out of the Park

The Making of Murder with an Axe

The Making of Death Day

The Making of Wonder

The Making of Canterbury Bound

The Making of Ospringe

The Making of Vesuvius Dominus

The Making of The Ninth Immersion

The Making of The Cornerstone of the Universe

The Making of The Only Person Alive in the World

The Making of Somewhere the Hurting Must Stop

The Making of Full of Scorpions is My Mind

The Making of Out West

The Making of Glenn Gould: Light and Dark

The Making of Emily Brontë: More Myself Than I

The Making of L. M. Montgomery: I Gave You Life

The Making of Pauline Johnson: Know Who I Am

The Making of John Passfield: Saturday Morning

The Making of Eleonora Duse: Let Me Have My Wings

The Making of James McIntyre: The Mammoth Cheese

The Making of Shakespeare and Cleopatra: My Life Is Not My Own

The Making of John and Santa: The Cowboy Shirt

The Making of John and Cassandra: Fair is Fair

The Making of John and Dickens: A Christmas Mystery

The Making of John and Lewis Carroll :Wonder Fall

The Making of John and Mother Goose: The Carnival of Tales

The Making of John and the Universan: Nothing is Known

See www.johnpassfield.ca for free access.

The Novel as an Art-Form:
Planning Notebooks by John Passfield

Each planning notebook records the planning, writing, editing and polishing of each novel. Each notebook is an attempt to record, understand, and organize the vast cluster of thoughts which occur as one grapples with the various levels of organization which a clear yet complex work of art demands.

Planning Grave Song

Planning Jumbo

Planning Pinafore Park

Planning Water Lane

Planning Rain of Fire

Planning Victoria Day

Planning Flight is Possible

Planning The Valley of the Shadow

Planning Out of the Park

Planning Murder with an Axe

Planning Death Day

Planning Wonder

Planning Canterbury Bound

Planning Ospringe

Planning Vesuvius Dominus

Planning The Ninth Immersion

Planning The Cornerstone of the Universe

Planning The Only Person Alive in the World

Planning Somewhere the Hurting Must Stop

Planning Full of Scorpions is My Mind

Planning Out West

Planning Glenn Gould: Light and Dark

Planning Emily Brontë: More Myself Than I

Planning L. M. Montgomery: I Gave You Life

Planning Pauline Johnson: Know Who I Am

Planning John Passfield: Saturday Morning

Planning Eleonora Duse: Let Me Have My Wings

Planning James McIntyre: The Mammoth Cheese

Planning Shakespeare and Cleopatra: My Life Is Not My Own

Planning John and Santa: The Cowboy Shirt

Planning John and Cassandra: Fair is Fair

Planning John and Dickens: A Christmas Mystery

Planning John and Lewis Carroll : Wonder Fall

Planning John and Mother Goose: The Carnival of Tales

Planning John and the Universan: Nothing is Known

See www.johnpassfield.ca for free access.

Other Books
by John Passfield

Oak Street
The Passfield Family

The Poetic Novel I
Influences and Elements

Intensities I
Verses on Various Topics

Intensities II
Verses on Various Topics

Deepening Imagery I
Verses from the Novels

Deepening Imagery II
Verses from the Novels

Deepening Imagery III
Verses from the Novels

Deepening Imagery IV
Verses from the Novels

Video-notes I
(1-100)

Video-notes II
(101-200)

See www.johnpassfield.ca for free access.